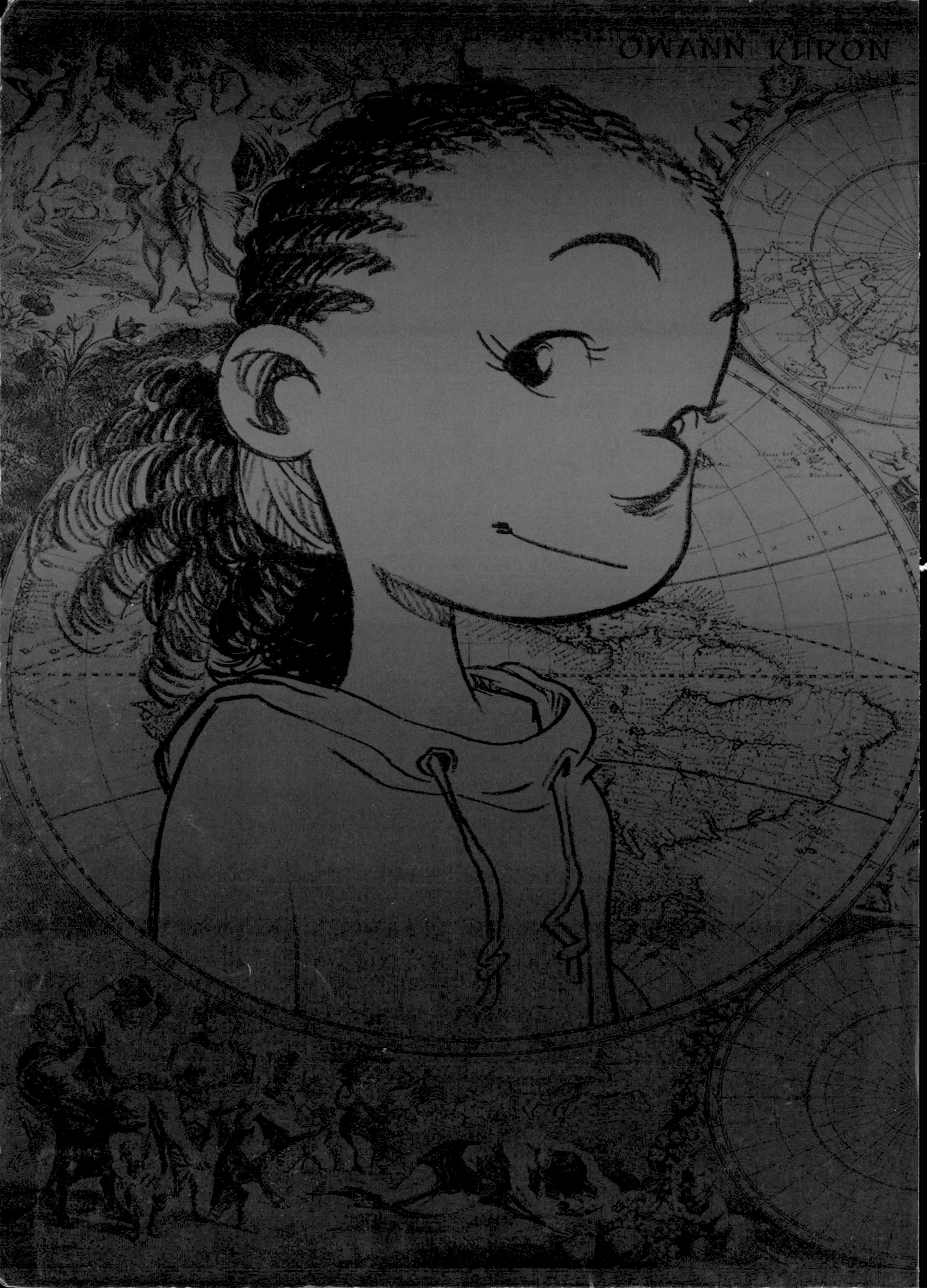
OWANN KURON

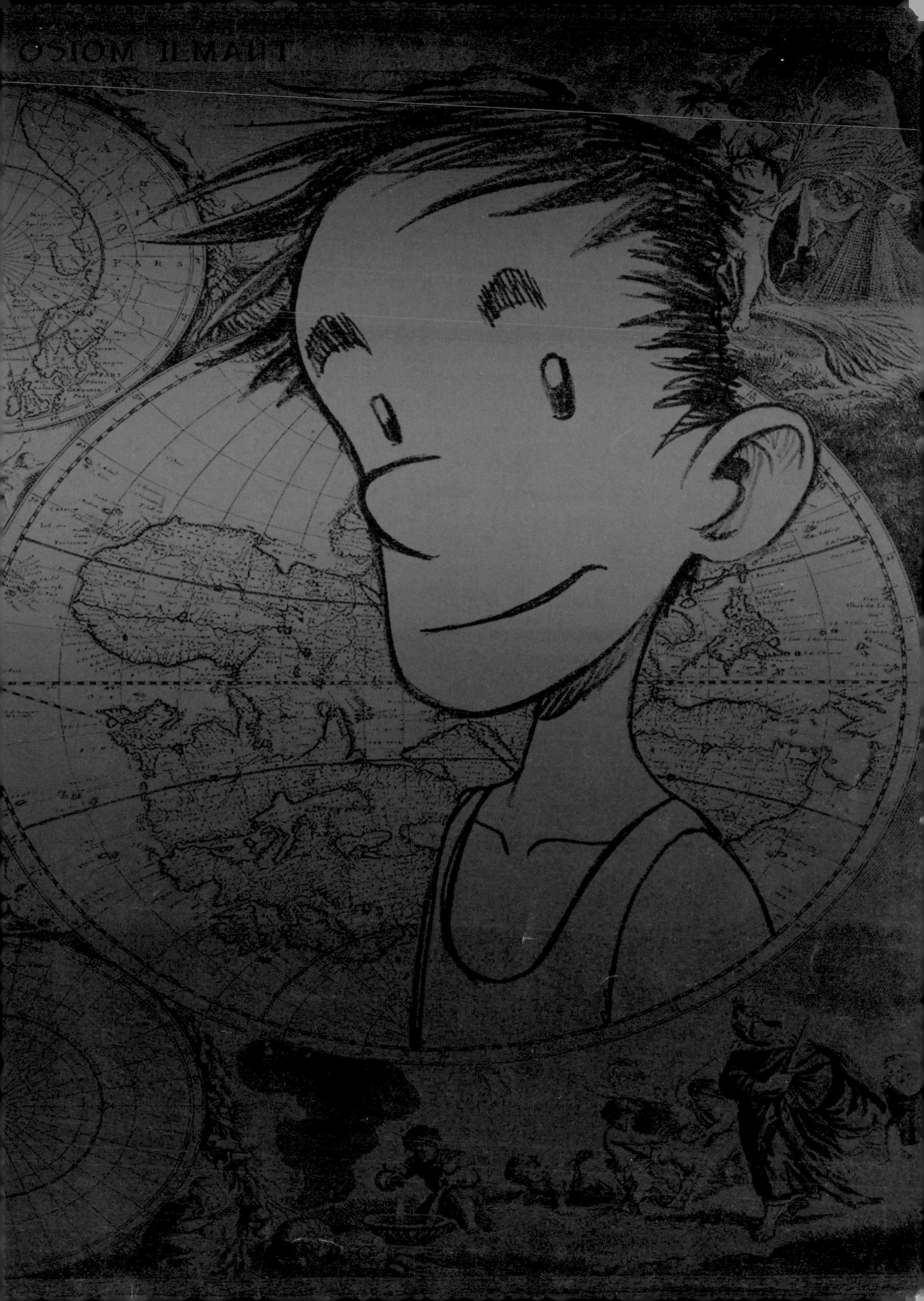

the ElseWhere CHRONICLES

BOOK THREE
THE MASTER OF SHADOWS

ART
BANNISTER

STORY
NYKKO

COLORS
JAFFRÉ

GRAPHIC UNIVERSE™ · MINNEAPOLIS · NEW YORK

Leaving Ilvanna and Norgavol behind, Rebecca and Max continue their journey, while Theo and Noah come through the passageway.

After an eventful arrival, Theo and Noah are welcomed by Ilvanna's village.

With the help of Doleann and her dragon Minervale, they catch up with Rebecca and Max in the ancient abandoned city of Themar, where they successfully escape a new attack from the Shadow Spies . . .

. . . but the Master of Shadows is at their heels.

Nykko and Corentin, bravo for toughing it out this far.
Flora, thank you for supporting us from day to day but most of all for the cakes.

—Bannister

To my wife, Sabine, and my children, Léo and Noé.
To Andrée, who has left us to explore another world.

—Nykko

Thank you very much, Mathilde, for being by my side and
for your help with the coloring!

—Jaffré

A very big thank you to Laurence and Denis, two great editors
without whom none of this would have been possible.
And thanks to Carol for her help and work on this current version.

—The Authors

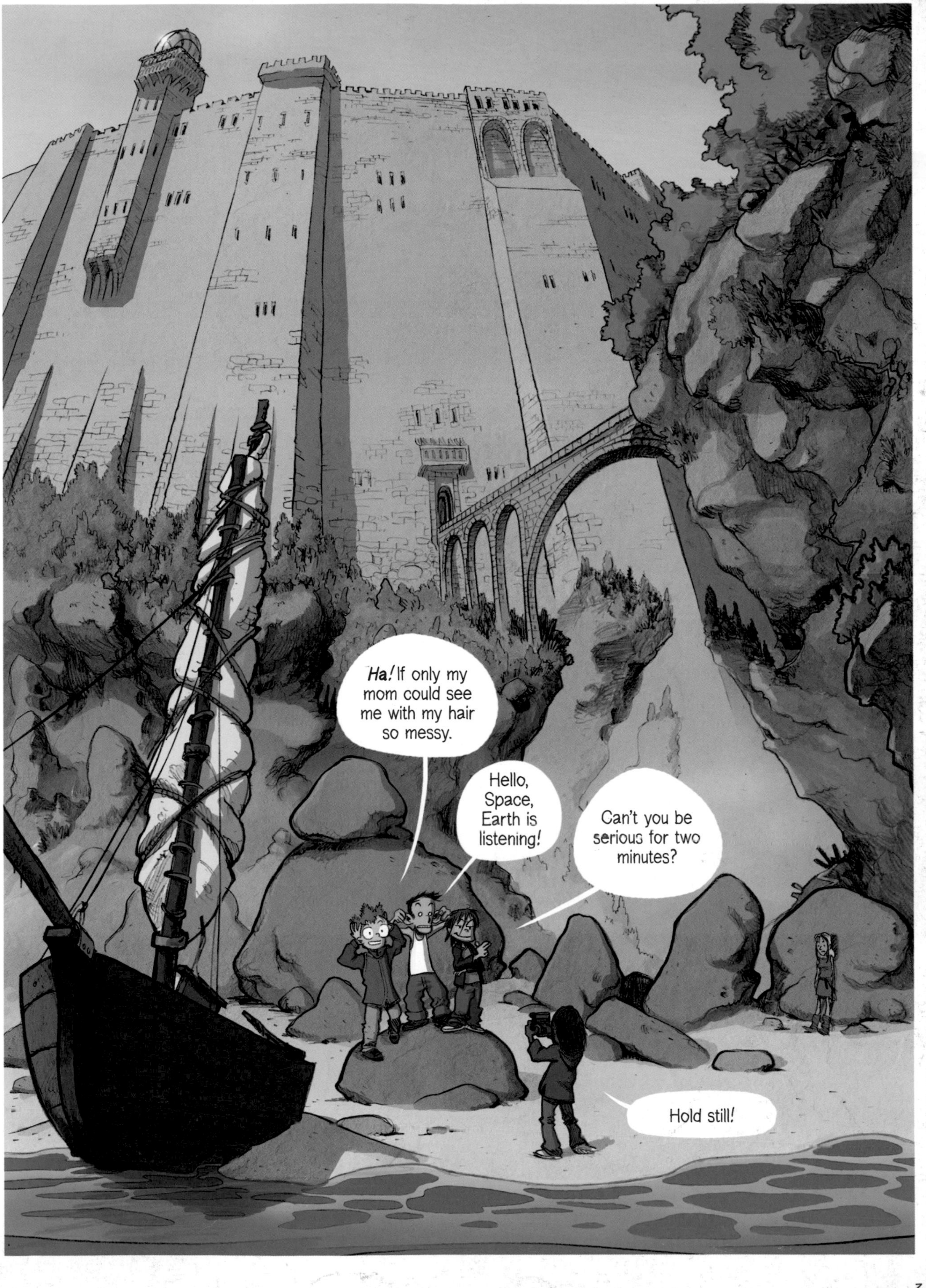
Ha! If only my mom could see me with my hair so messy.
Hello, Space, Earth is listening!
Can't you be serious for two minutes?
Hold still!

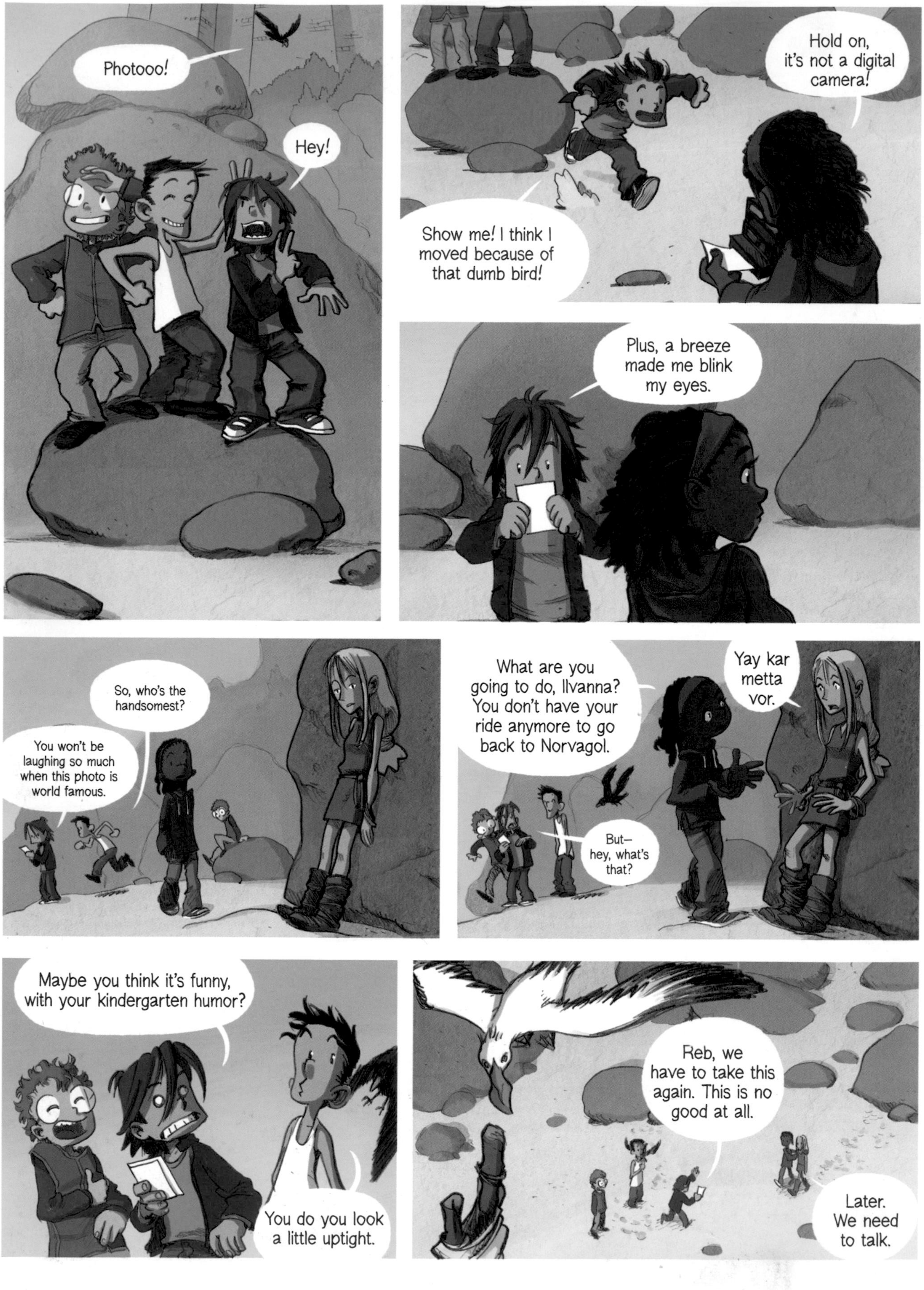
Photooo!
Hey!
Hold on, it's not a digital camera!
Show me! I think I moved because of that dumb bird!
Plus, a breeze made me blink my eyes.
So, who's the handsomest?
You won't be laughing so much when this photo is world famous.
What are you going to do, Ilvanna? You don't have your ride anymore to go back to Norvagol.
Yay kar metta vor.
But— hey, what's that?
Maybe you think it's funny, with your kindergarten humor?
You do you look a little uptight.
Reb, we have to take this again. This is no good at all.
Later. We need to talk.

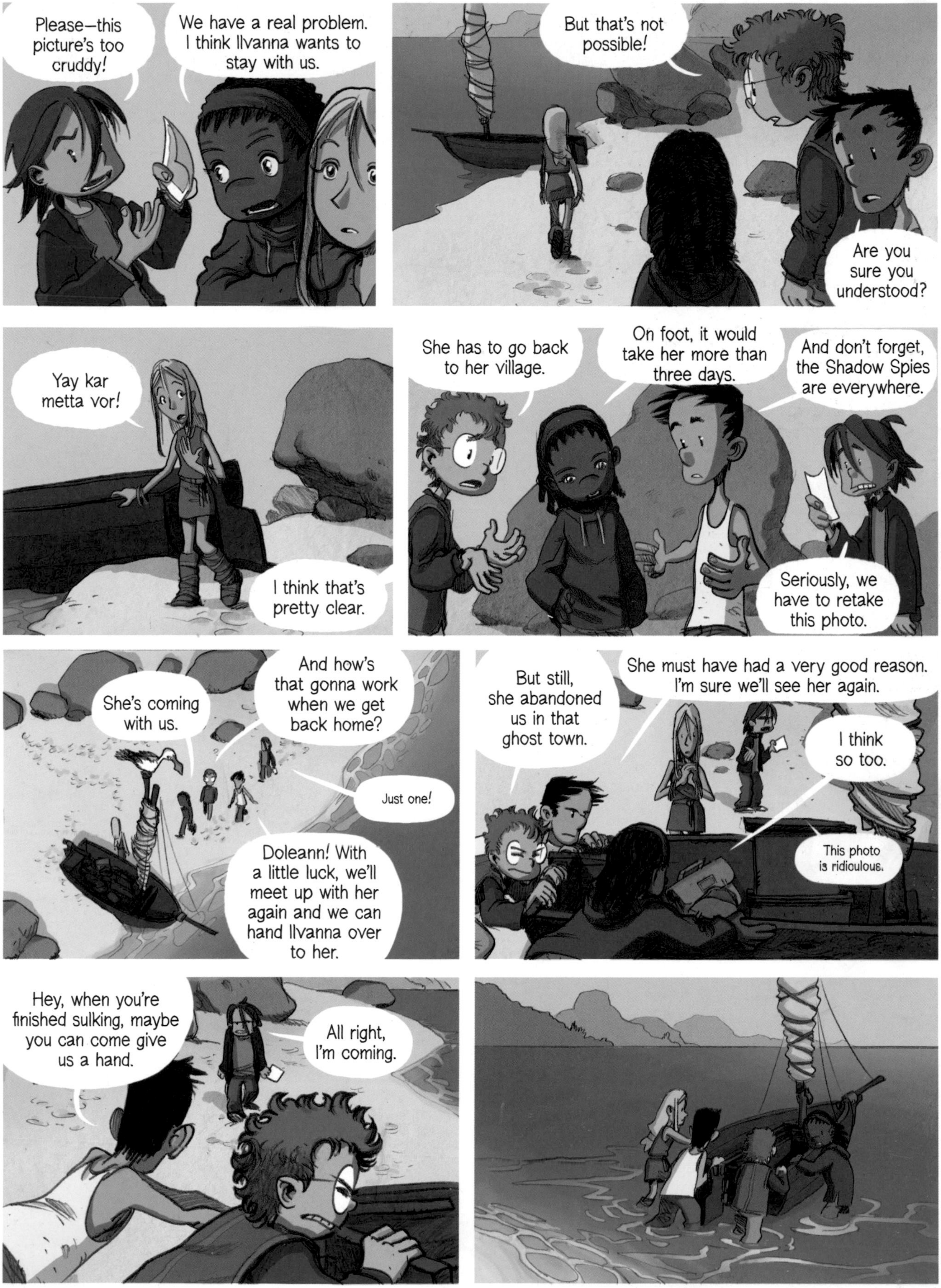
Please—this picture's too cruddy!
We have a real problem. I think Ilvanna wants to stay with us.
But that's not possible!
Are you sure you understood?
Yay kar metta vor!
I think that's pretty clear.
She has to go back to her village.
On foot, it would take her more than three days.
And don't forget, the Shadow Spies are everywhere.
Seriously, we have to retake this photo.
She's coming with us.
And how's that gonna work when we get back home?
Just one!
Doleann! With a little luck, we'll meet up with her again and we can hand Ilvanna over to her.
But still, she abandoned us in that ghost town.
She must have had a very good reason. I'm sure we'll see her again.
I think so too.
This photo is ridiculous.
Hey, when you're finished sulking, maybe you can come give us a hand.
All right, I'm coming.

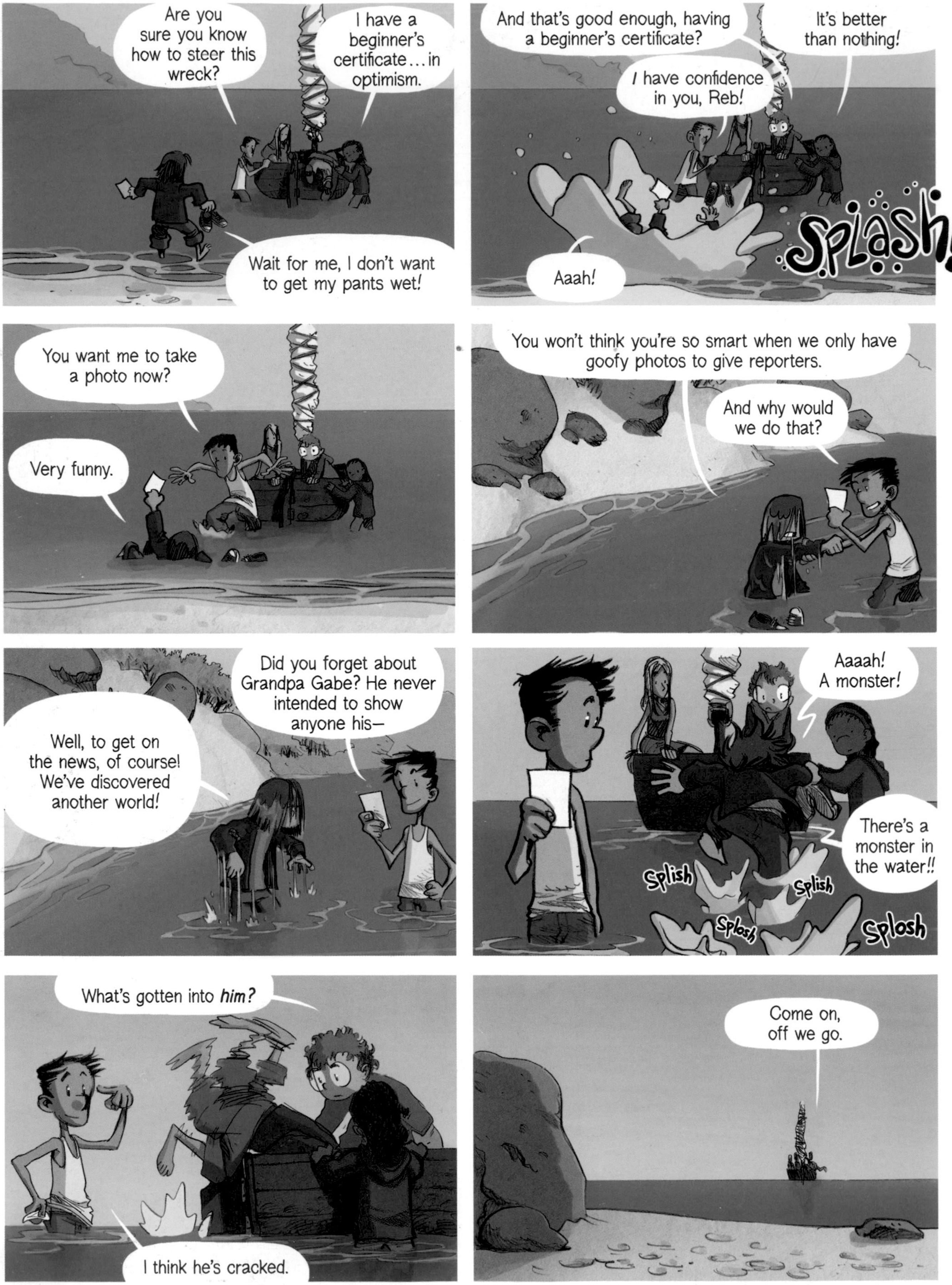
Are you sure you know how to steer this wreck?
I have a beginner's certificate... in optimism.
Wait for me, I don't want to get my pants wet!
And that's good enough, having a beginner's certificate?
It's better than nothing!
I have confidence in you, Reb!
Aaah!
SPLASH!
You want me to take a photo now?
Very funny.
You won't think you're so smart when we only have goofy photos to give reporters.
And why would we do that?
Did you forget about Grandpa Gabe? He never intended to show anyone his–
Well, to get on the news, of course! We've discovered another world!
Aaaah! A monster!
There's a monster in the water!!
Splish
Splish
Splosh
Splosh
What's gotten into him?
I think he's cracked.
Come on, off we go.

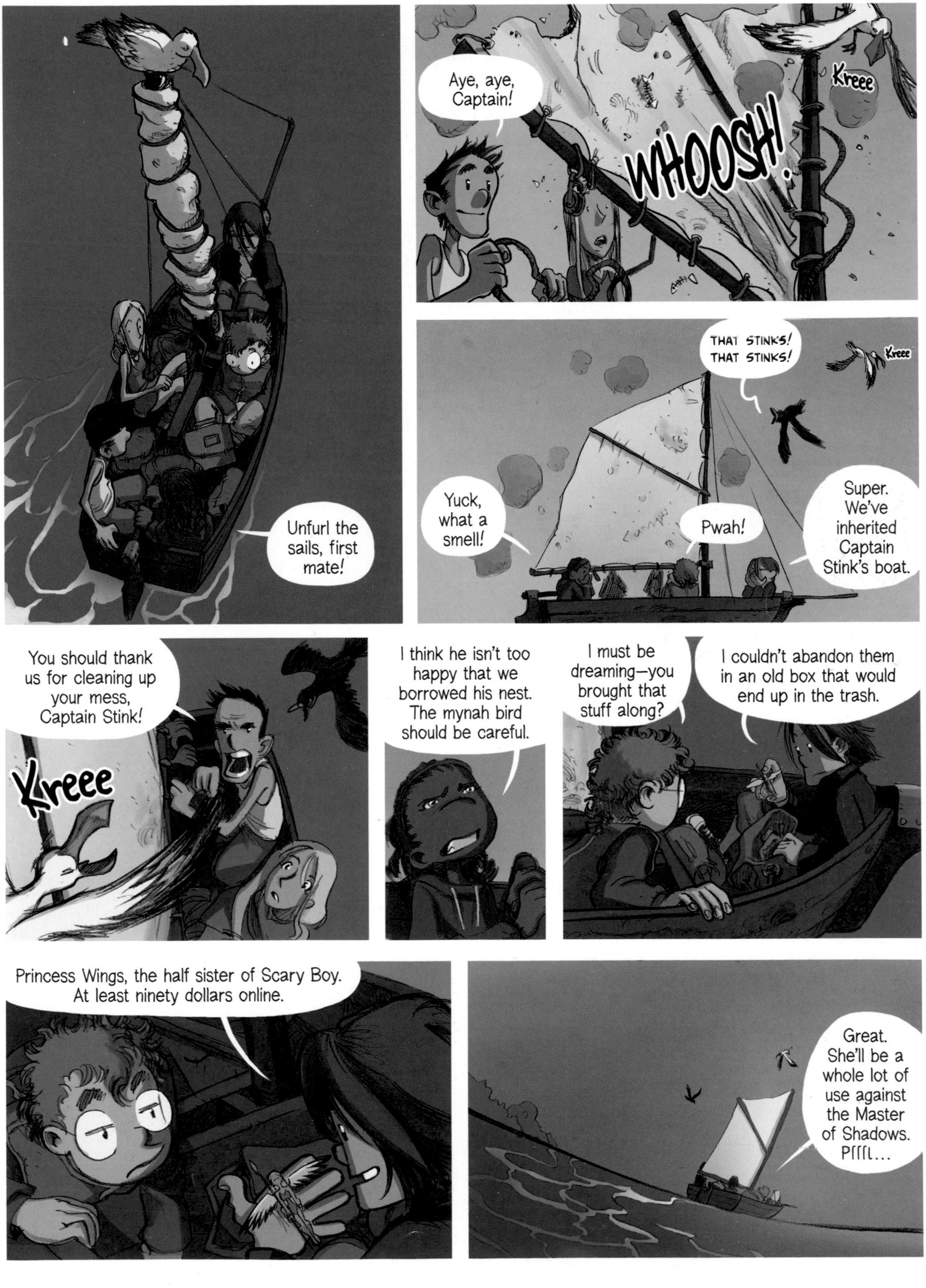
Unfurl the sails, first mate!
Aye, aye, Captain!
WHOOSH!
Kreee
THAT STINKS! THAT STINKS!
Kreee
Yuck, what a smell!
Pwah!
Super. We've inherited Captain Stink's boat.
You should thank us for cleaning up your mess, Captain Stink!
Kreee
I think he isn't too happy that we borrowed his nest. The mynah bird should be careful.
I must be dreaming—you brought that stuff along?
I couldn't abandon them in an old box that would end up in the trash.
Princess Wings, the half sister of Scary Boy. At least ninety dollars online.
Great. She'll be a whole lot of use against the Master of Shadows. Pffff...

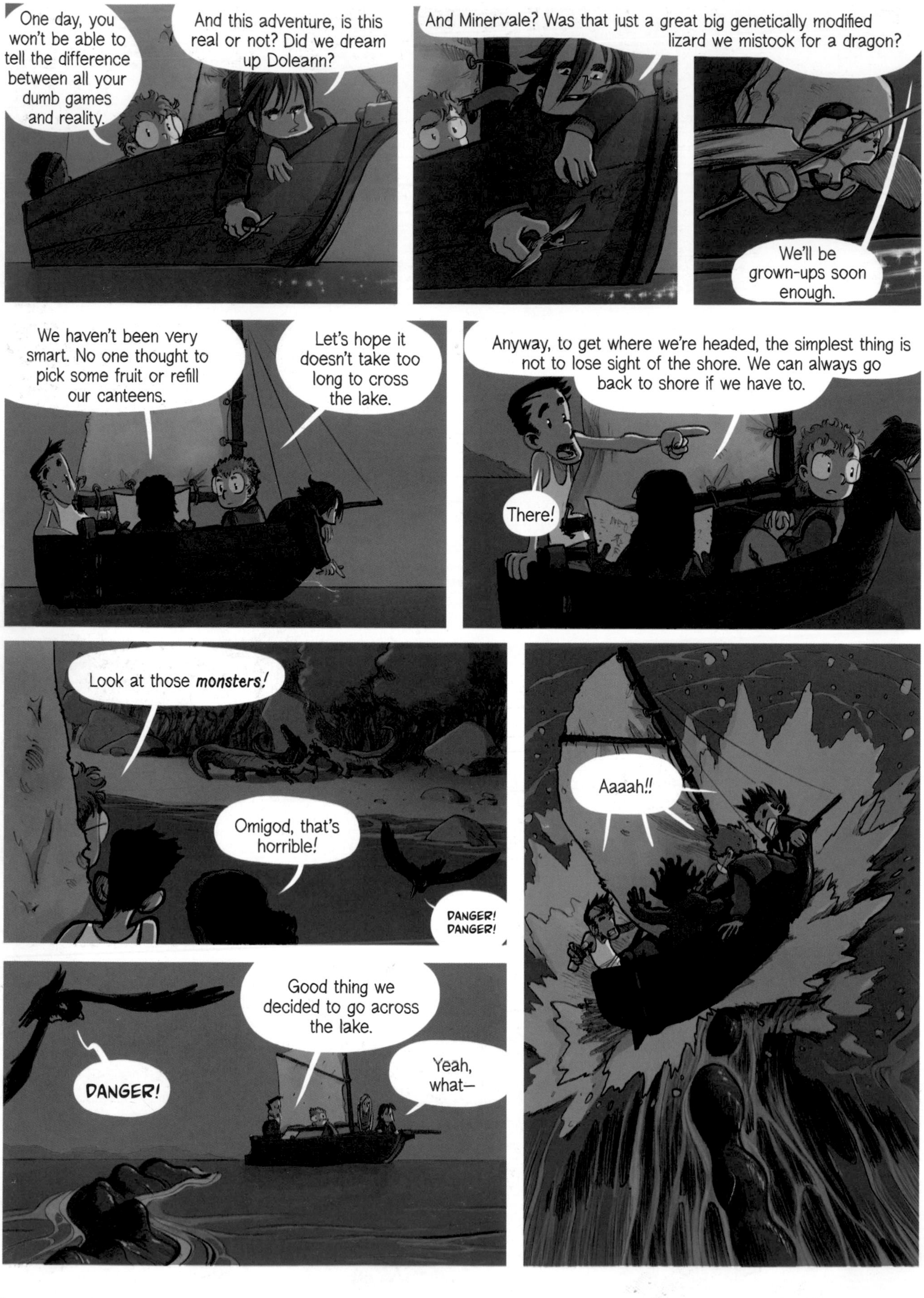

One day, you won't be able to tell the difference between all your dumb games and reality.
And this adventure, is this real or not? Did we dream up Doleann?
And Minervale? Was that just a great big genetically modified lizard we mistook for a dragon?
We'll be grown-ups soon enough.
We haven't been very smart. No one thought to pick some fruit or refill our canteens.
Let's hope it doesn't take too long to cross the lake.
Anyway, to get where we're headed, the simplest thing is not to lose sight of the shore. We can always go back to shore if we have to.
There!
Look at those *monsters!*
Omigod, that's horrible!
DANGER! DANGER!
Good thing we decided to go across the lake.
DANGER!
Yeah, what—
Aaaah!!

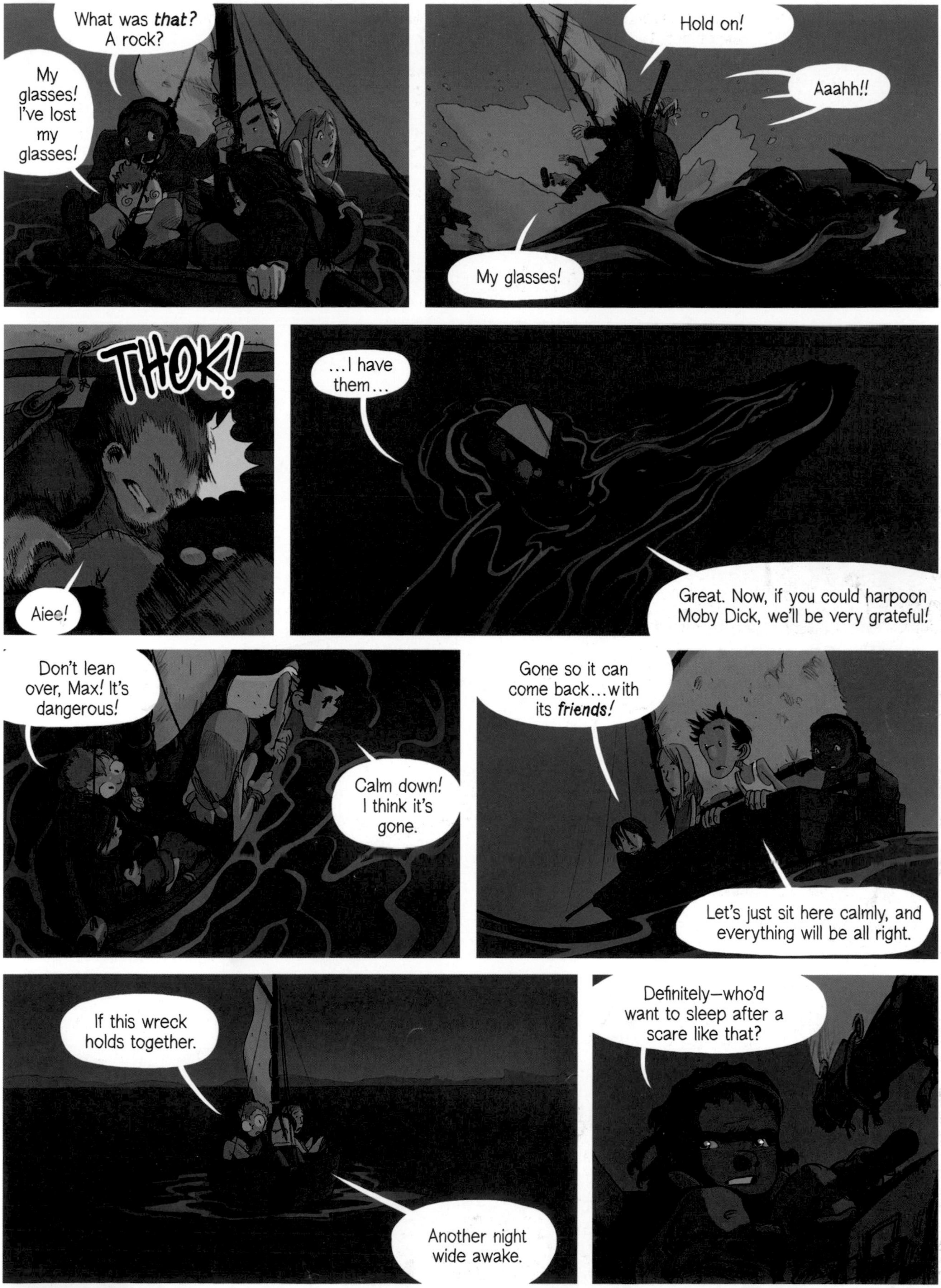
What was *that?* A rock?
My glasses! I've lost my glasses!
Hold on!
Aaahh!!
My glasses!
THOK!
Aiee!
...I have them...
Great. Now, if you could harpoon Moby Dick, we'll be very grateful!
Don't lean over, Max! It's dangerous!
Calm down! I think it's gone.
Gone so it can come back...with its *friends!*
Let's just sit here calmly, and everything will be all right.
If this wreck holds together.
Another night wide awake.
Definitely—who'd want to sleep after a scare like that?

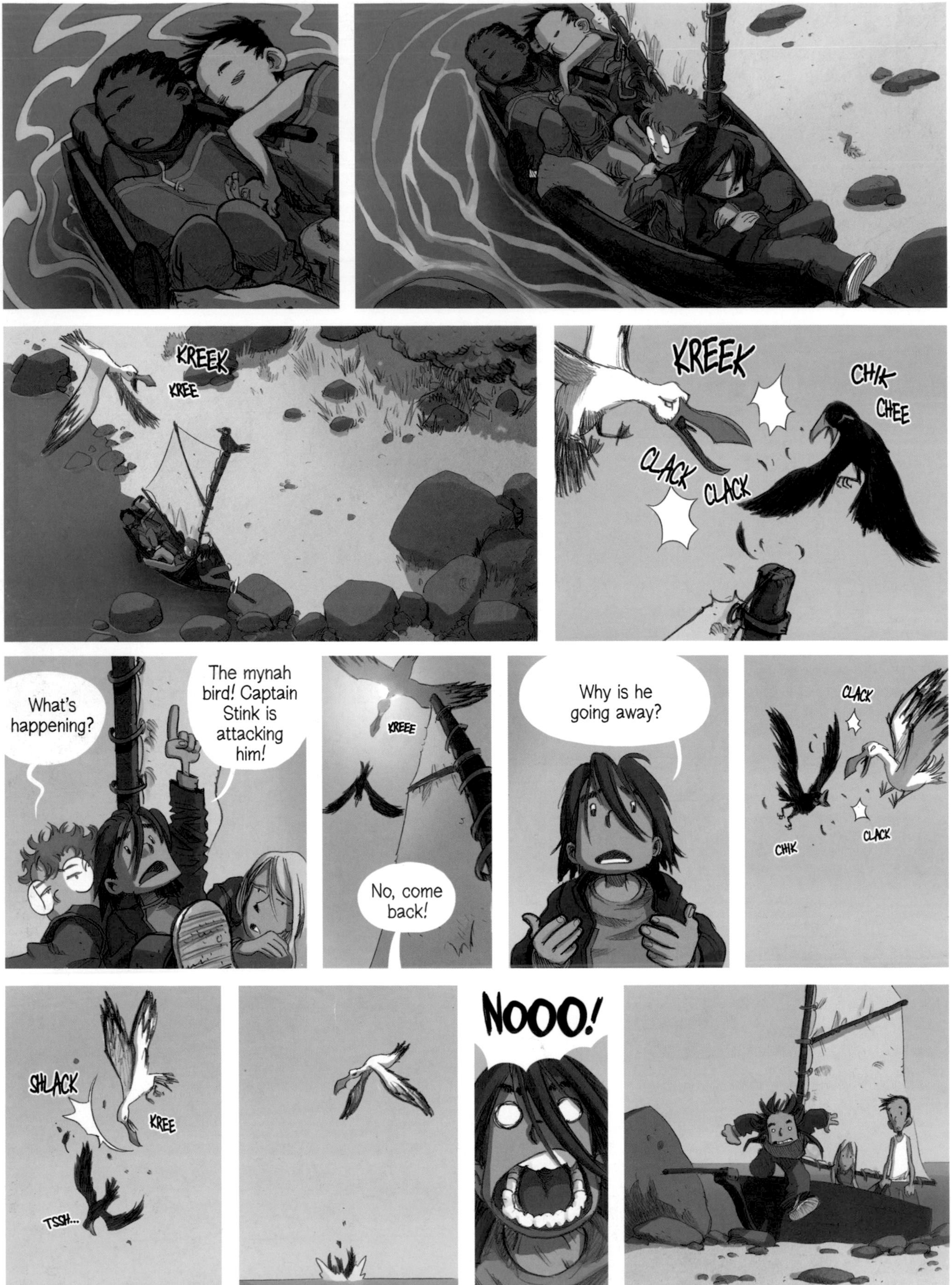

KREEK
KREE
KREEK
CHIK
CHEE
CLACK
CLACK
What's happening?
The mynah bird! Captain Stink is attacking him!
KREEE
No, come back!
Why is he going away?
CLACK
CHIK
CLACK
SHLACK
KREE
TSSH...
NOOO!

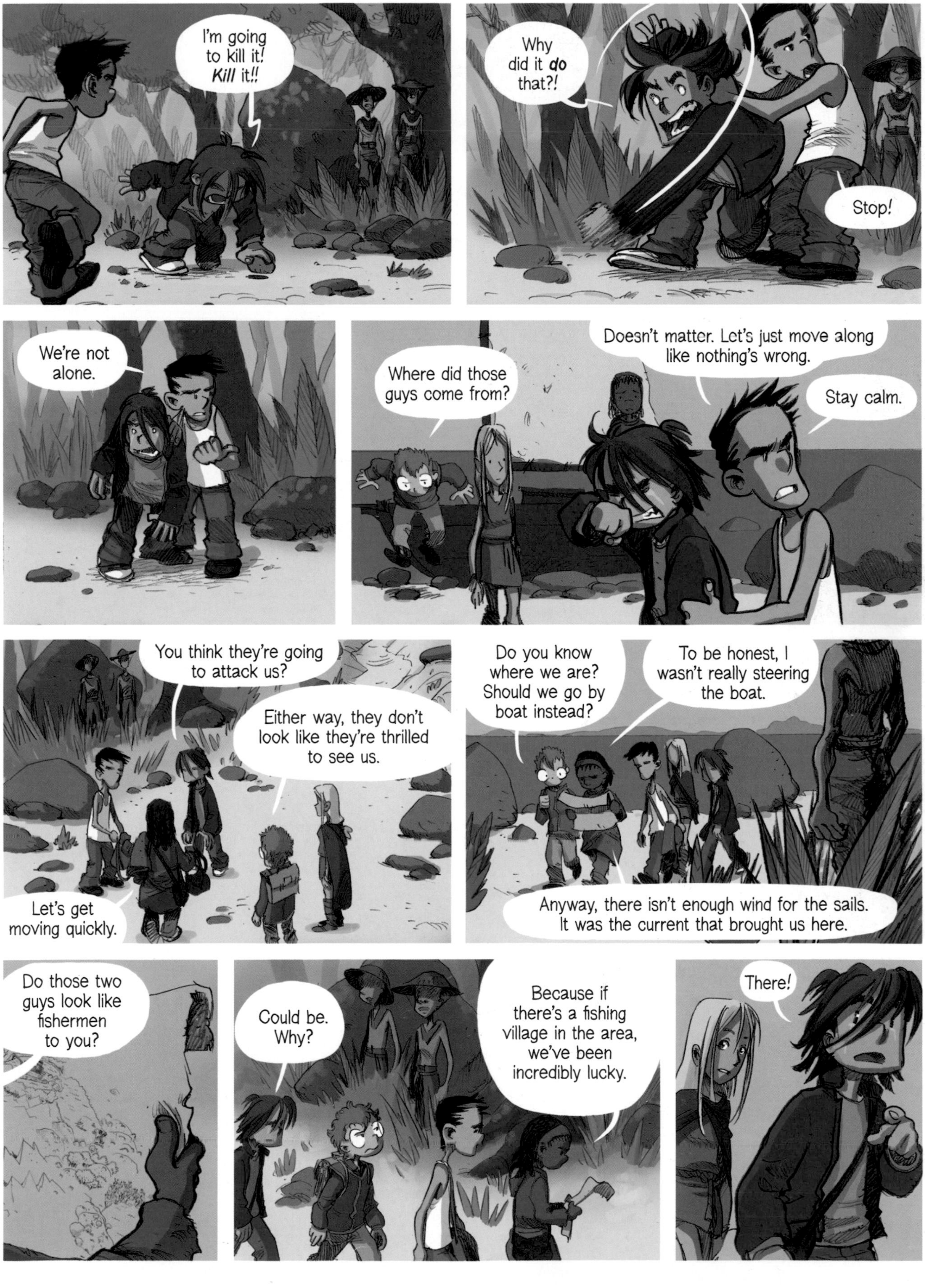
I'm going to kill it! *Kill* it!!
Why did it *do* that?!
Stop!
We're not alone.
Where did those guys come from?
Doesn't matter. Let's just move along like nothing's wrong.
Stay calm.
You think they're going to attack us?
Either way, they don't look like they're thrilled to see us.
Let's get moving quickly.
Do you know where we are? Should we go by boat instead?
To be honest, I wasn't really steering the boat.
Anyway, there isn't enough wind for the sails. It was the current that brought us here.
Do those two guys look like fishermen to you?
Could be. Why?
Because if there's a fishing village in the area, we've been incredibly lucky.
There!

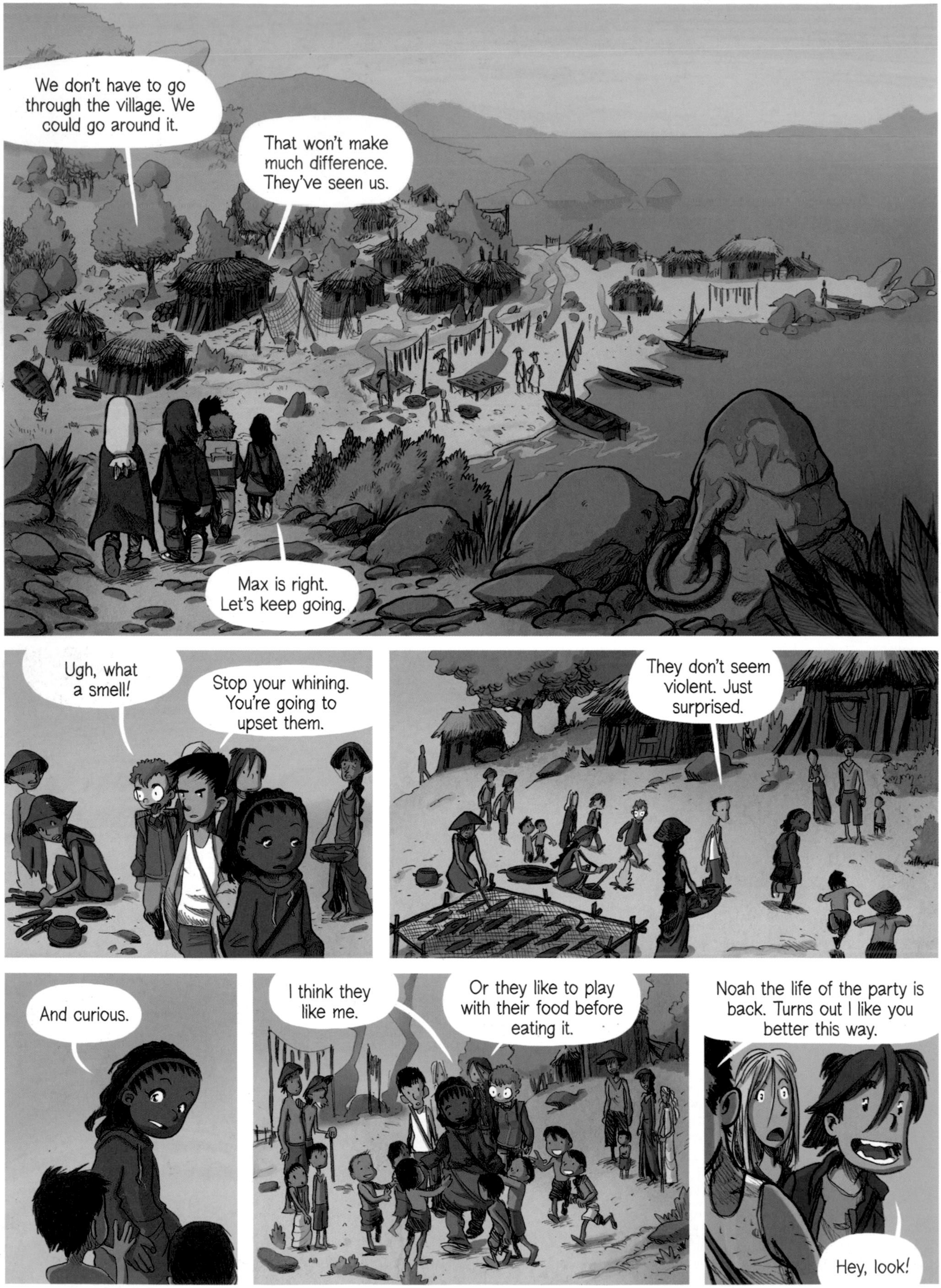
We don't have to go through the village. We could go around it.
That won't make much difference. They've seen us.
Max is right. Let's keep going.
Ugh, what a smell!
Stop your whining. You're going to upset them.
They don't seem violent. Just surprised.
And curious.
I think they like me.
Or they like to play with their food before eating it.
Noah the life of the party is back. Turns out I like you better this way.
Hey, look!

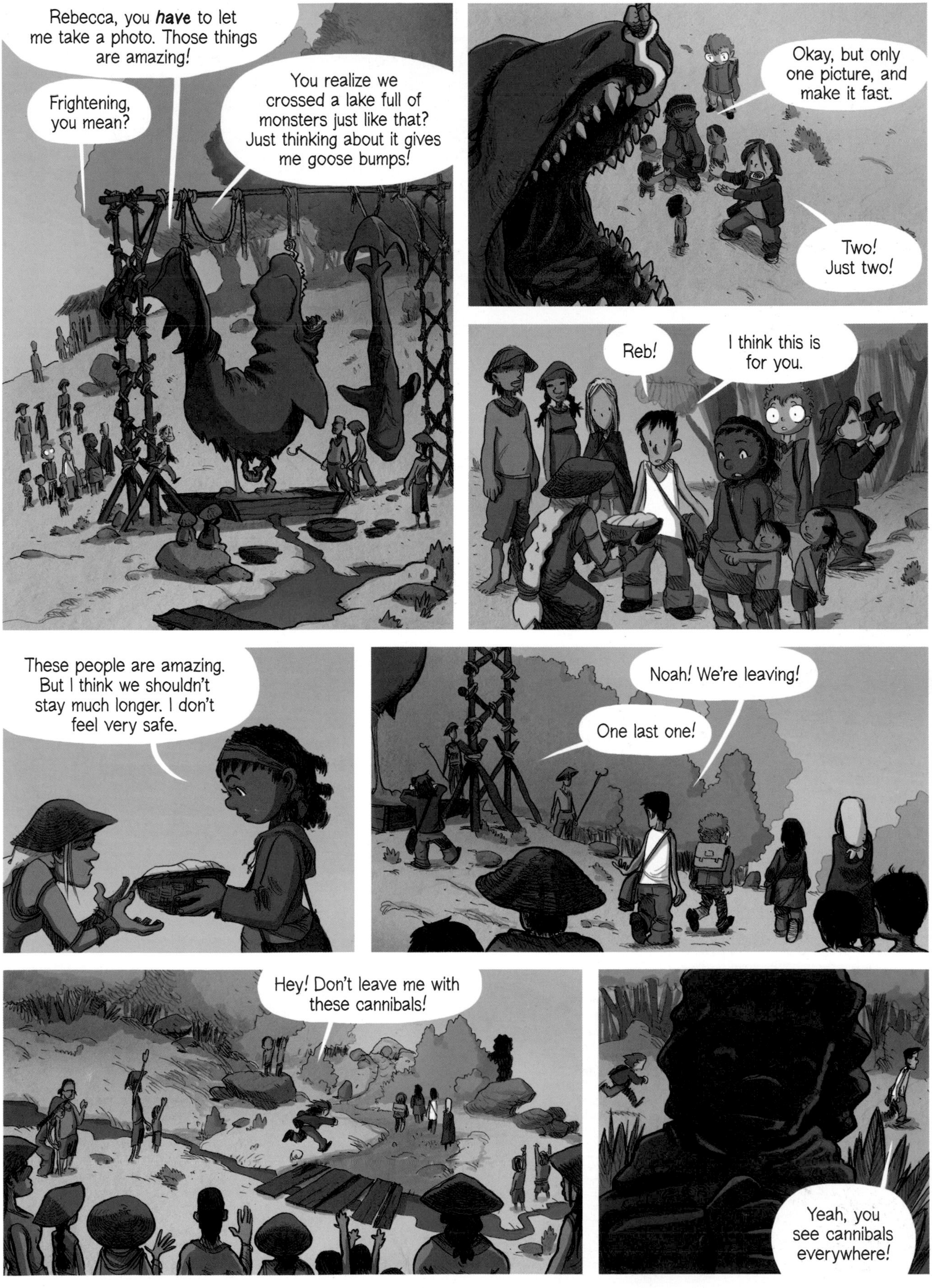
Rebecca, you **have** to let me take a photo. Those things are amazing!
Frightening, you mean?
You realize we crossed a lake full of monsters just like that? Just thinking about it gives me goose bumps!
Okay, but only one picture, and make it fast.
Two! Just two!
Reb!
I think this is for you.
These people are amazing. But I think we shouldn't stay much longer. I don't feel very safe.
Noah! We're leaving!
One last one!
Hey! Don't leave me with these cannibals!
Yeah, you see cannibals everywhere!

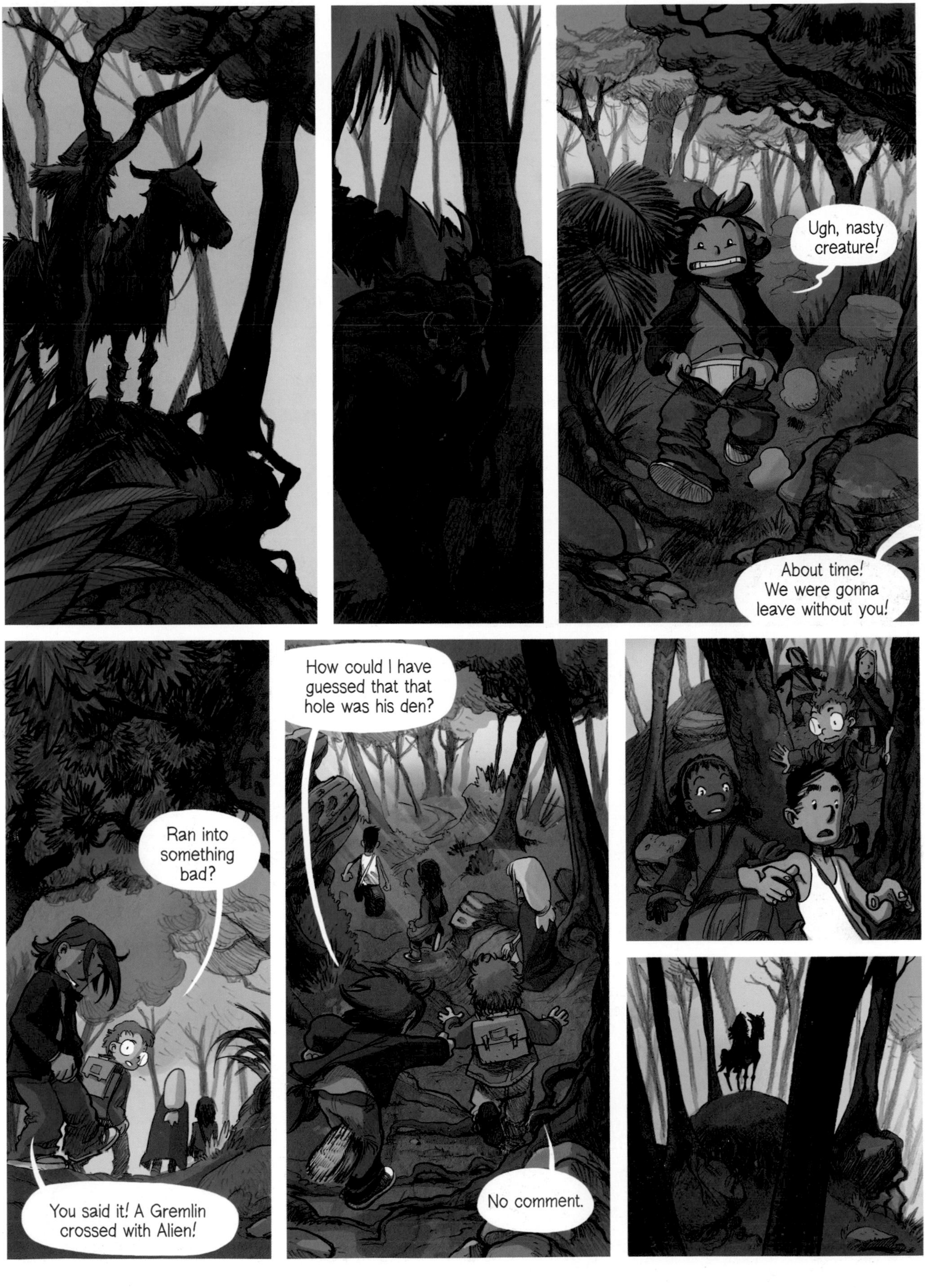
Ugh, nasty creature!
About time! We were gonna leave without you!
Ran into something bad?
You said it! A Gremlin crossed with Alien!
How could I have guessed that that hole was his den?
No comment.

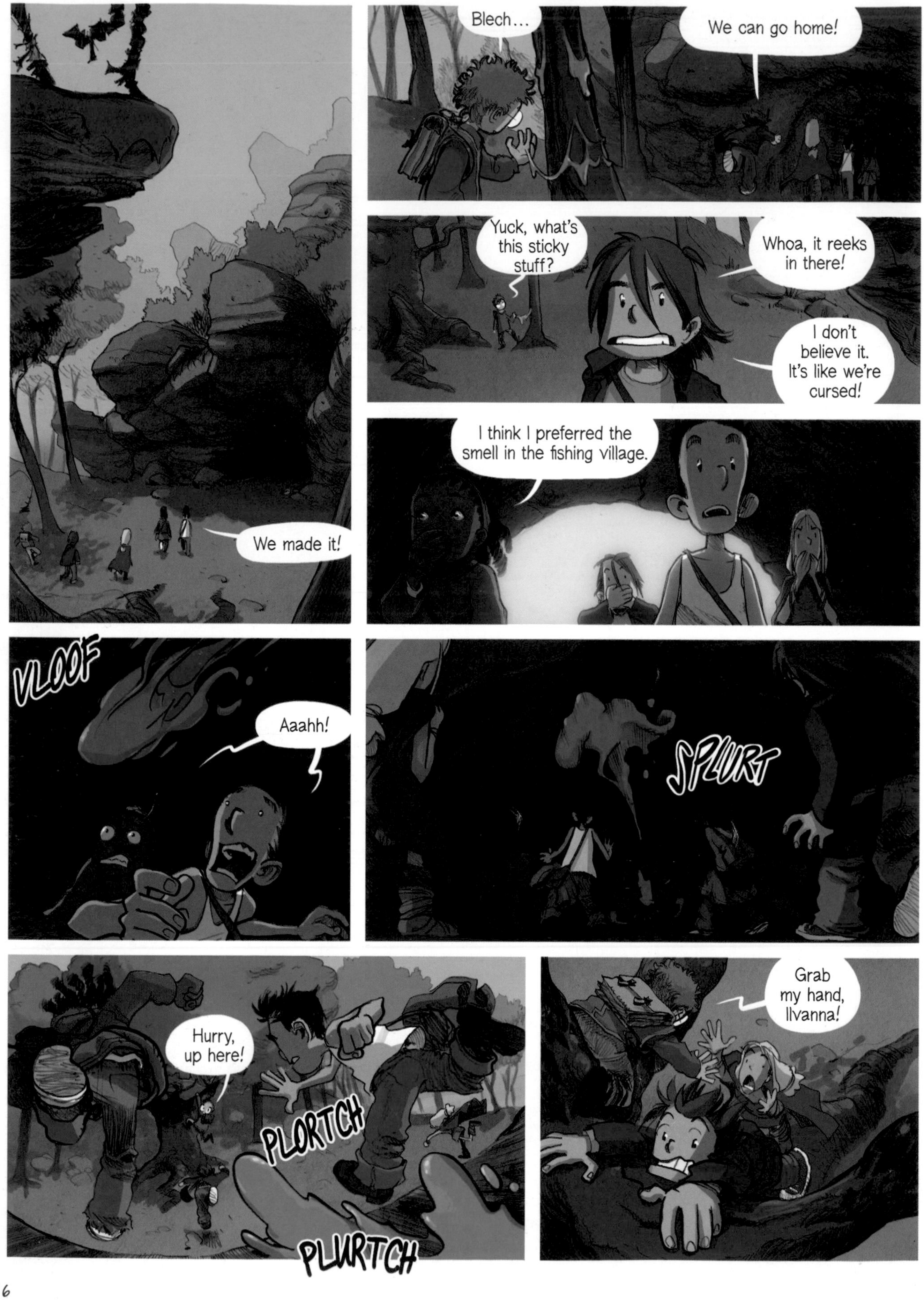
We made it!
Blech...
We can go home!
Yuck, what's this sticky stuff?
Whoa, it reeks in there!
I don't believe it. It's like we're cursed!
I think I preferred the smell in the fishing village.
VLOOF
Aaahh!
SPLURT
Hurry, up here!
PLORTCH
PLURTCH
Grab my hand, Ilvanna!

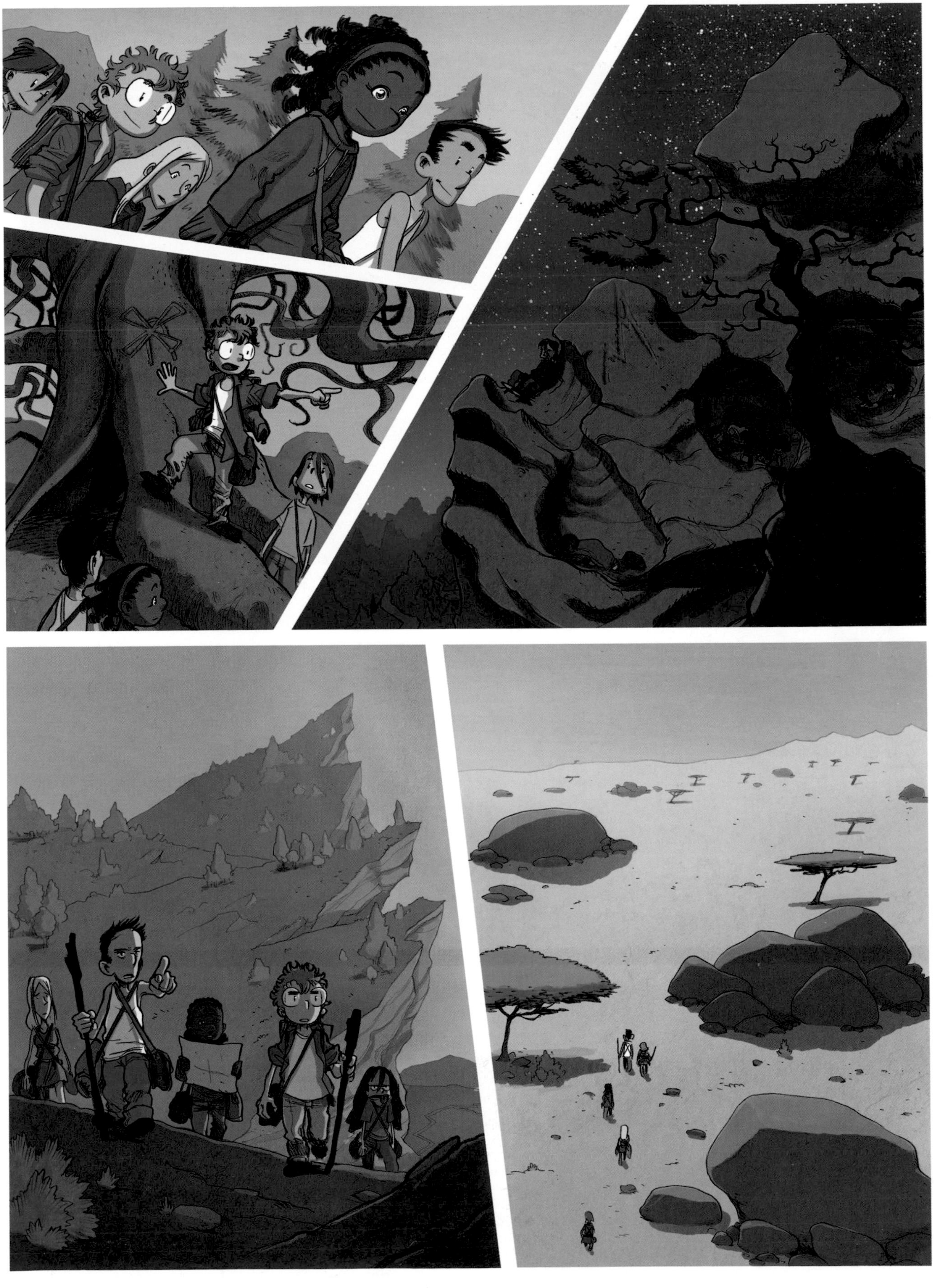

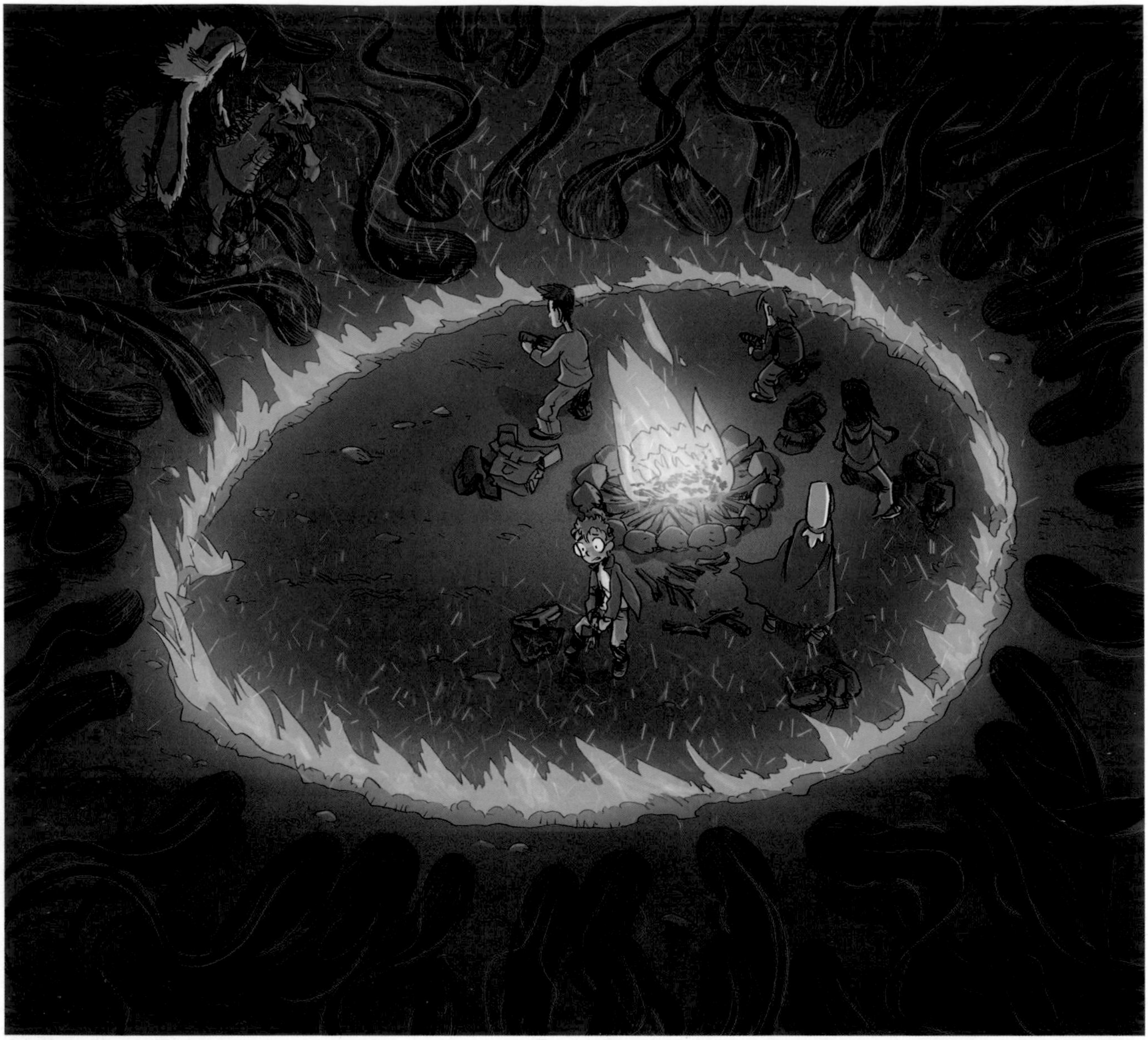

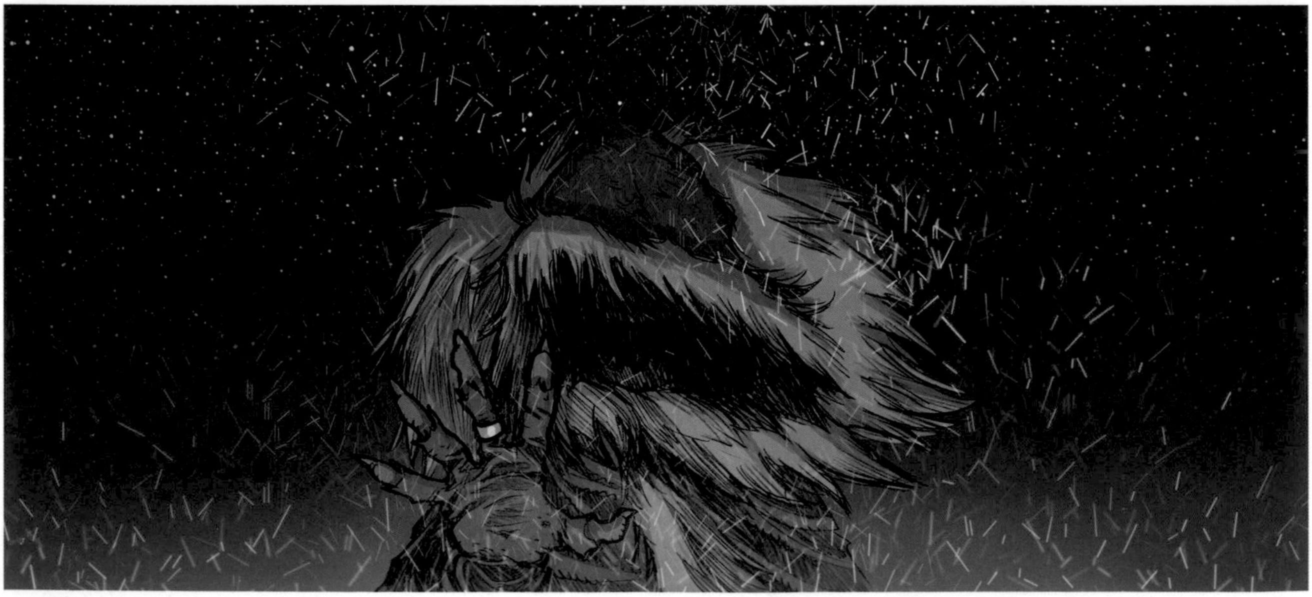

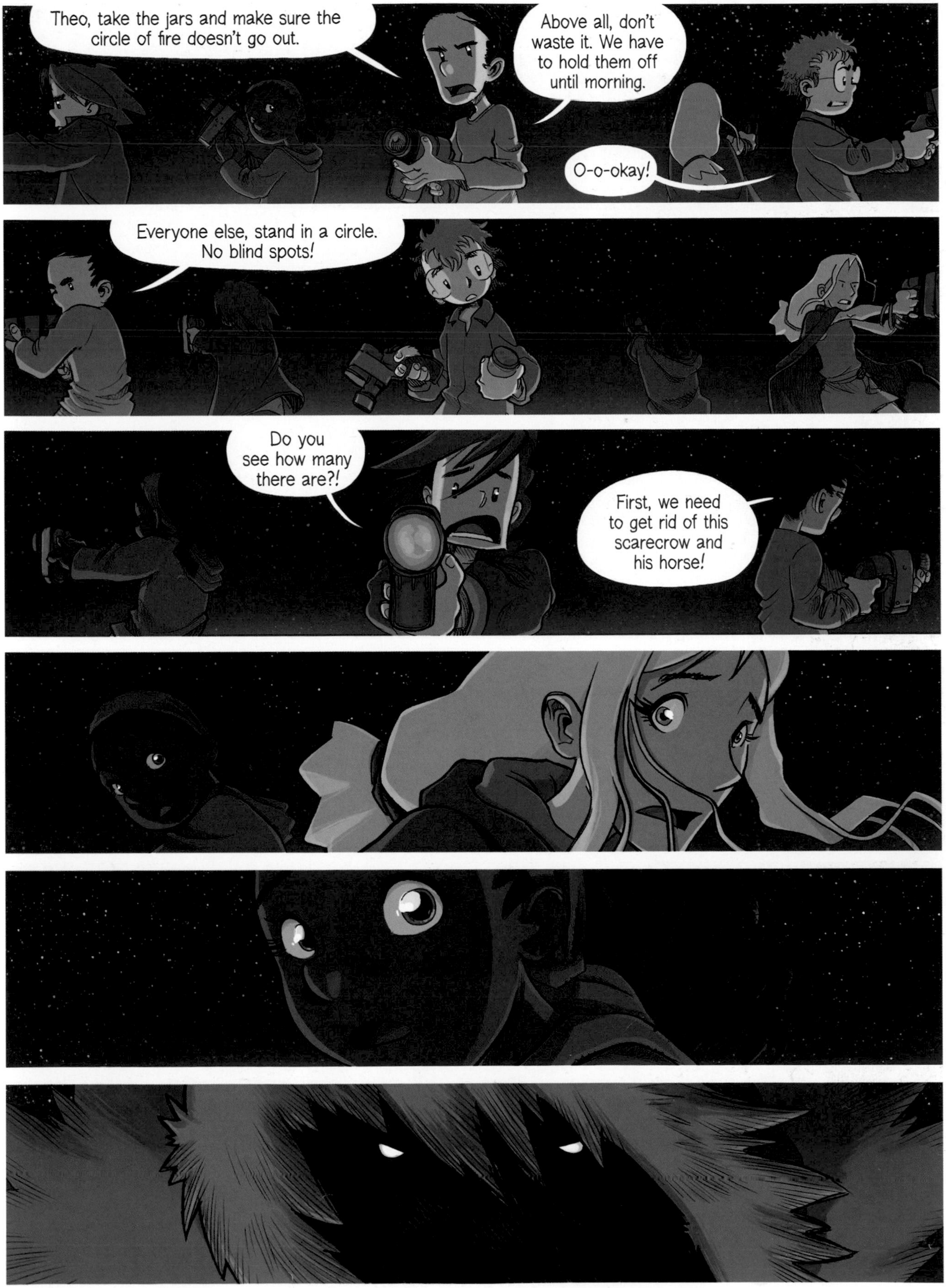

Theo, take the jars and make sure the circle of fire doesn't go out.
Above all, don't waste it. We have to hold them off until morning.
O-o-okay!
Everyone else, stand in a circle. No blind spots!
Do you see how many there are?!
First, we need to get rid of this scarecrow and his horse!

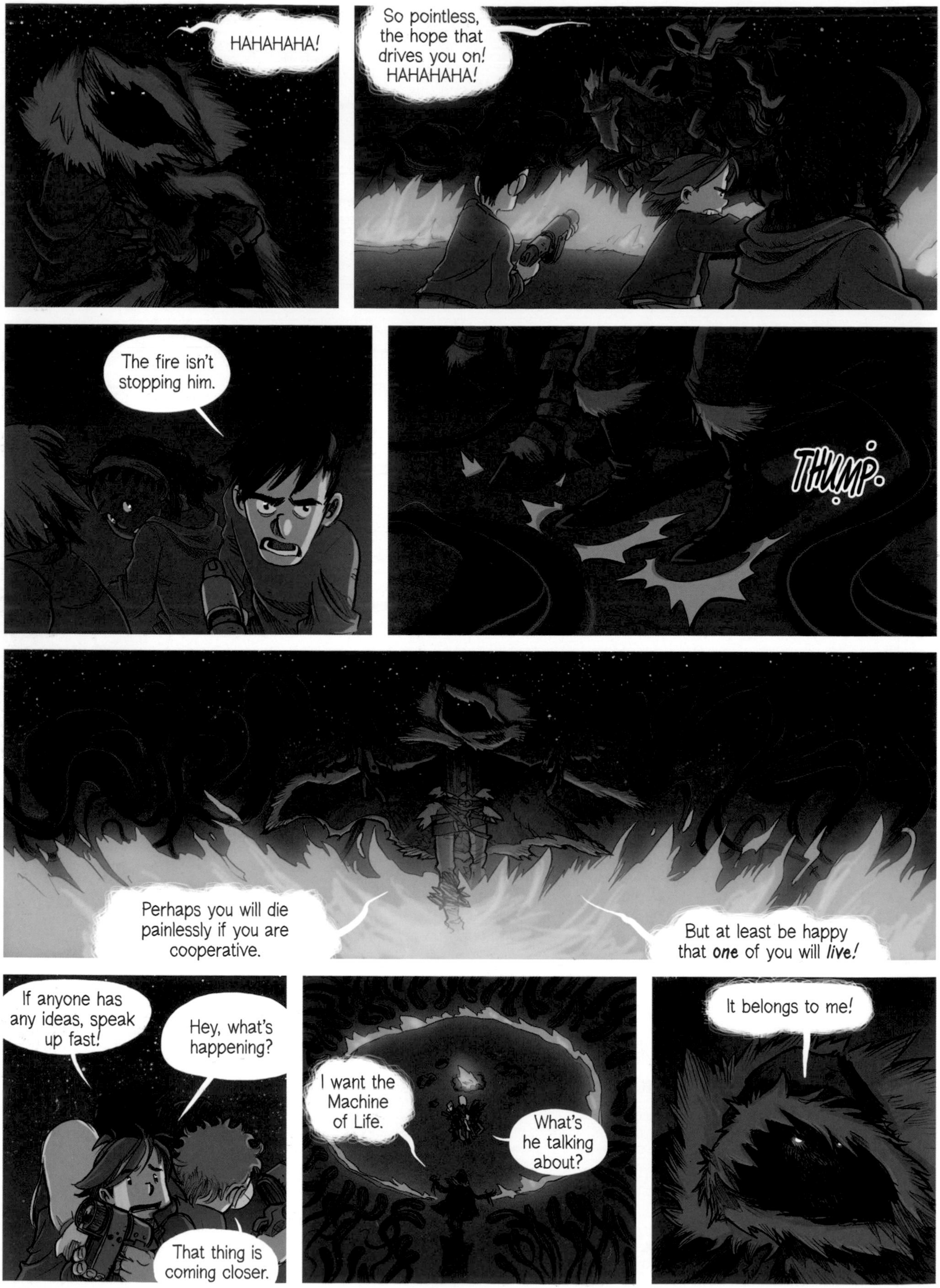
HAHAHAHA!
So pointless, the hope that drives you on! HAHAHAHA!
The fire isn't stopping him.
THUMP.
Perhaps you will die painlessly if you are cooperative.
But at least be happy that *one* of you will *live!*
If anyone has any ideas, speak up fast!
Hey, what's happening?
That thing is coming closer.
I want the Machine of Life.
What's he talking about?
It belongs to me!

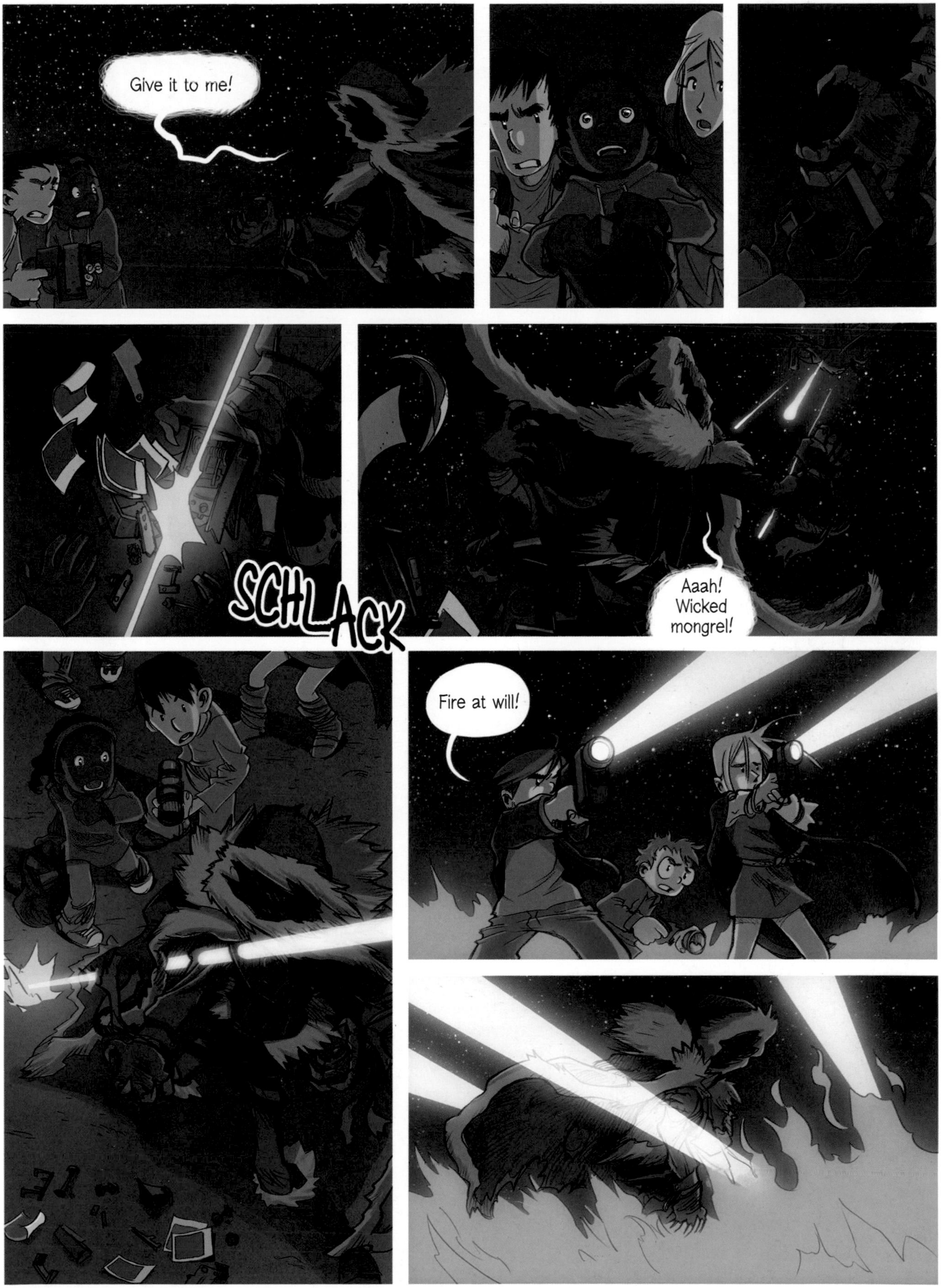
Give it to me!
SCHLACK
Aaah! Wicked mongrel!
Fire at will!

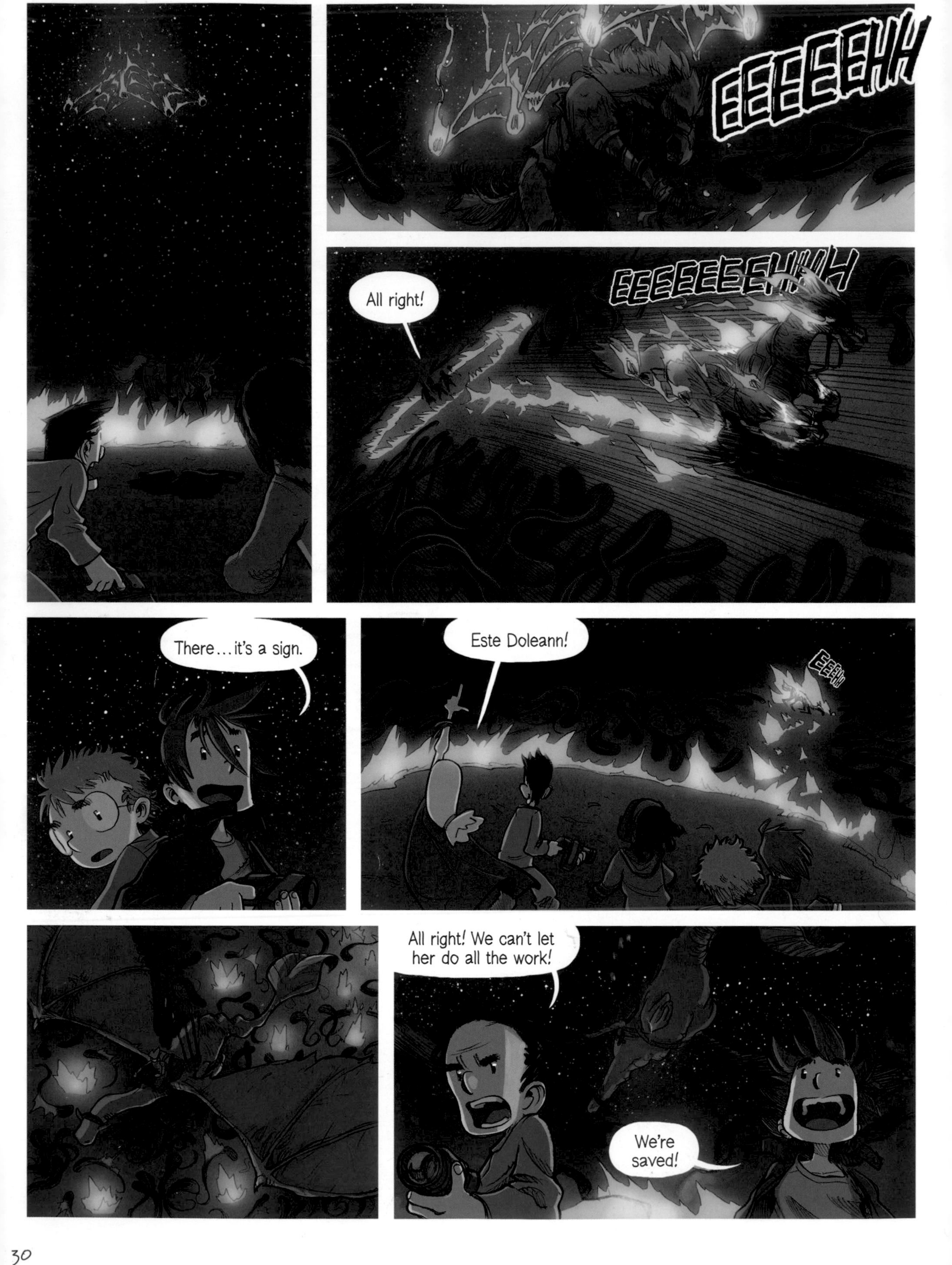
EEEEEHH
All right!
EEEEEEEEHHH
There...it's a sign.
Este Doleann!
All right! We can't let her do all the work!
We're saved!

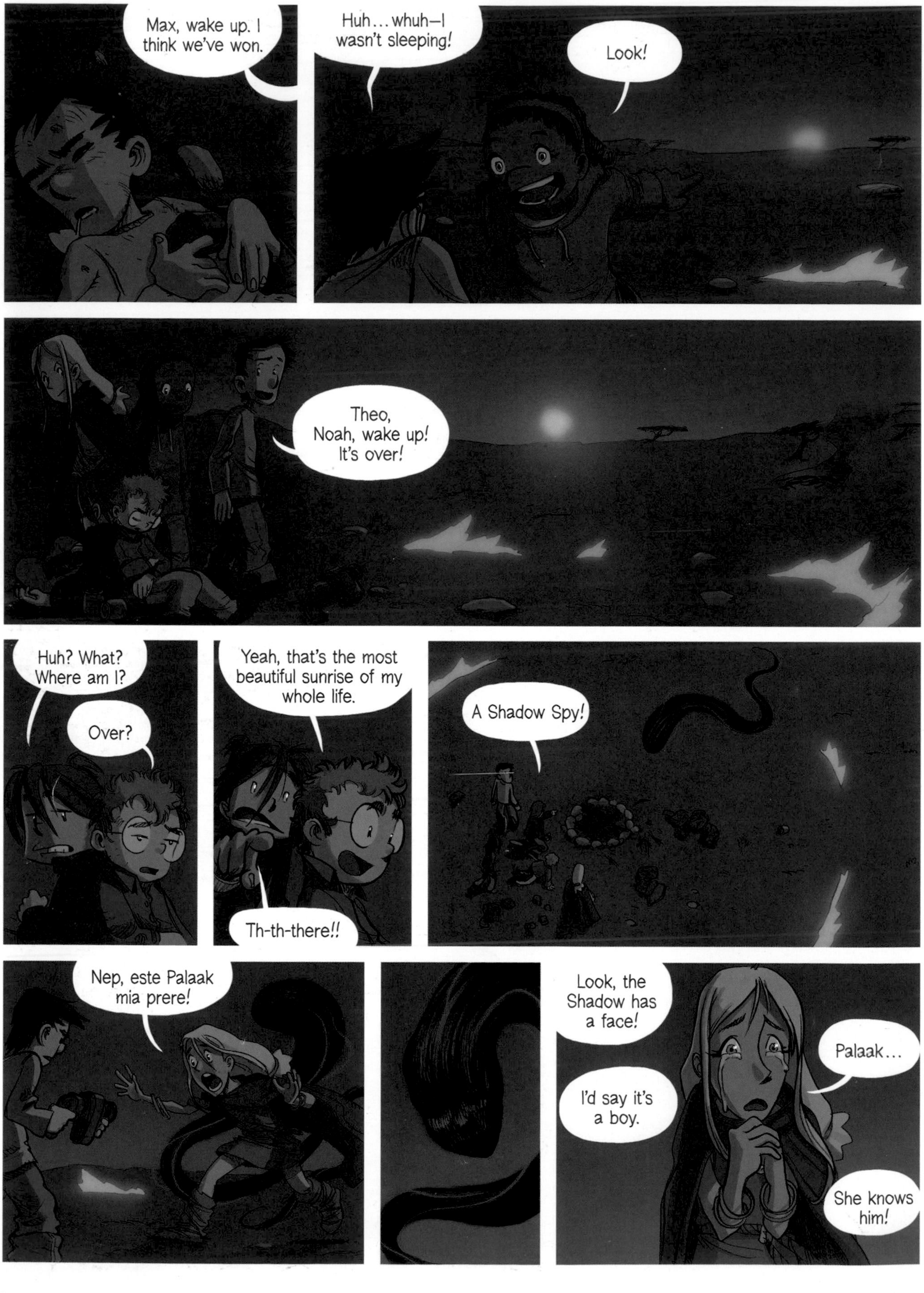

Max, wake up. I think we've won.
Huh...whuh—I wasn't sleeping!
Look!
Theo, Noah, wake up! It's over!
Huh? What? Where am I?
Over?
Yeah, that's the most beautiful sunrise of my whole life.
Th-th-there!!
A Shadow Spy!
Nep, este Palaak mia prere!
Look, the Shadow has a face!
I'd say it's a boy.
Palaak...
She knows him!

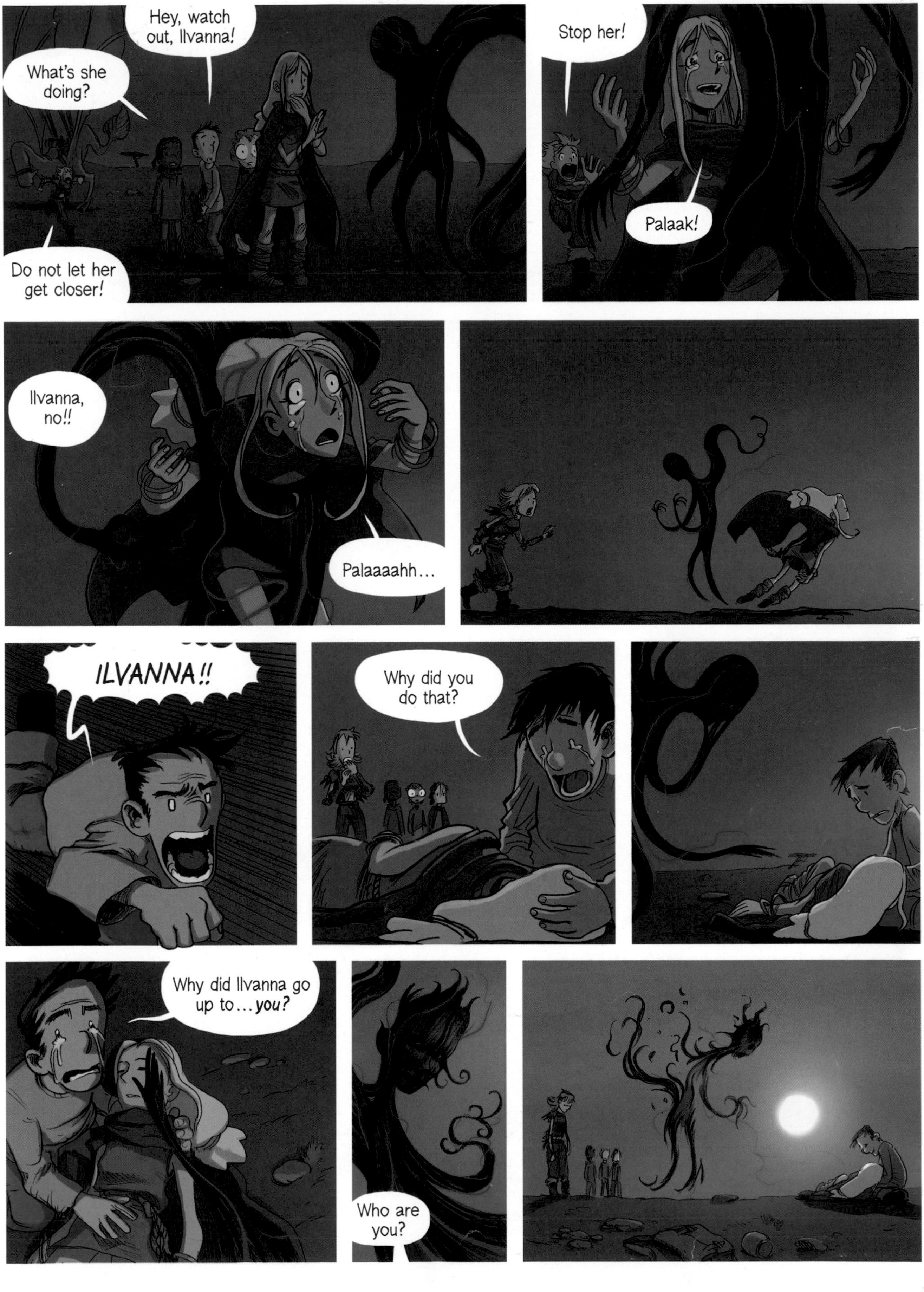
What's she doing?
Hey, watch out, Ilvanna!
Do not let her get closer!
Stop her!
Palaak!
Ilvanna, no!!
Palaaaahh...
ILVANNA!!
Why did you do that?
Why did Ilvanna go up to... *you?*
Who are you?

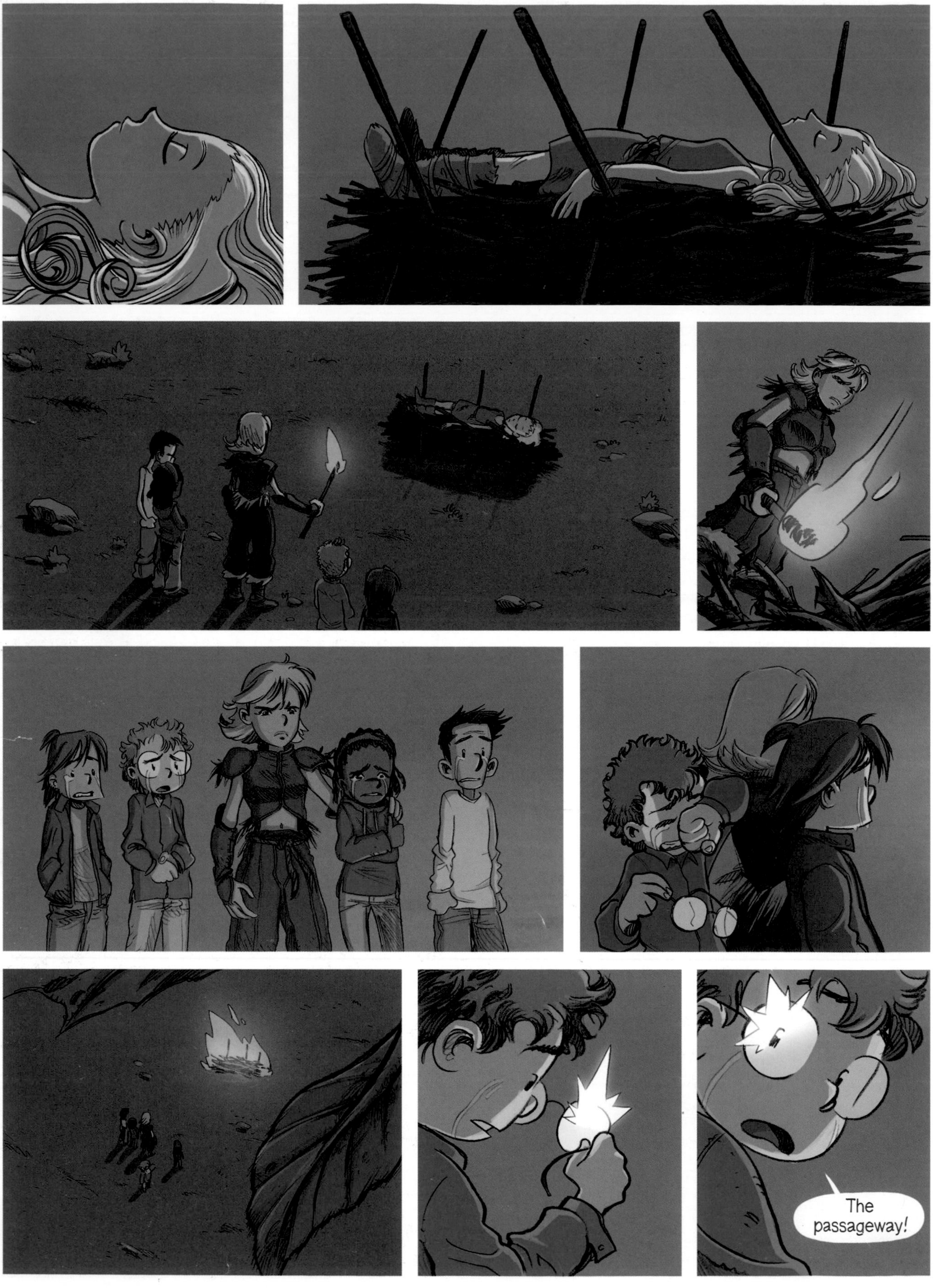
The passageway!

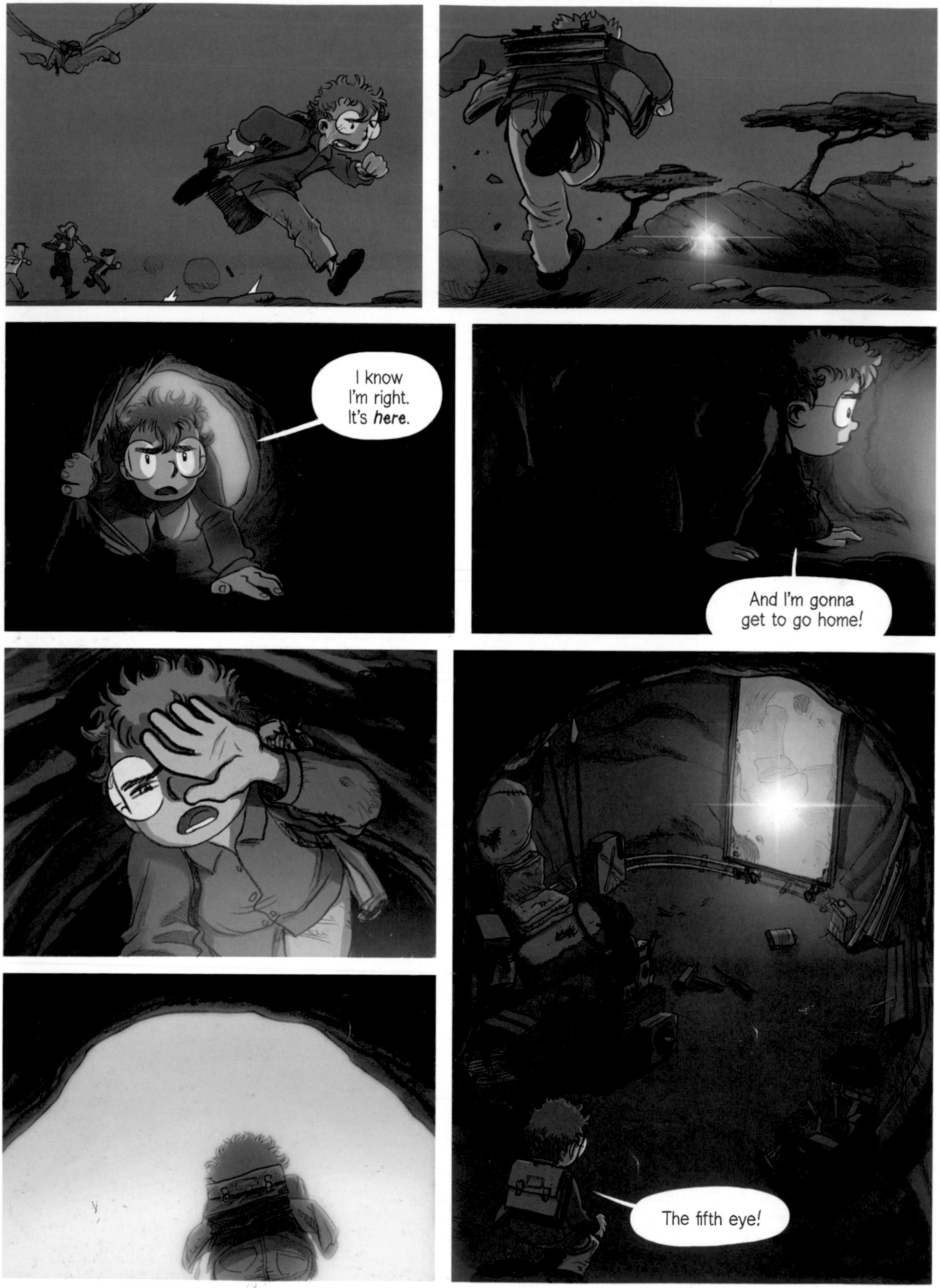
I know
I'm right.
It's *here*.
And I'm gonna
get to go home!
The fifth eye!

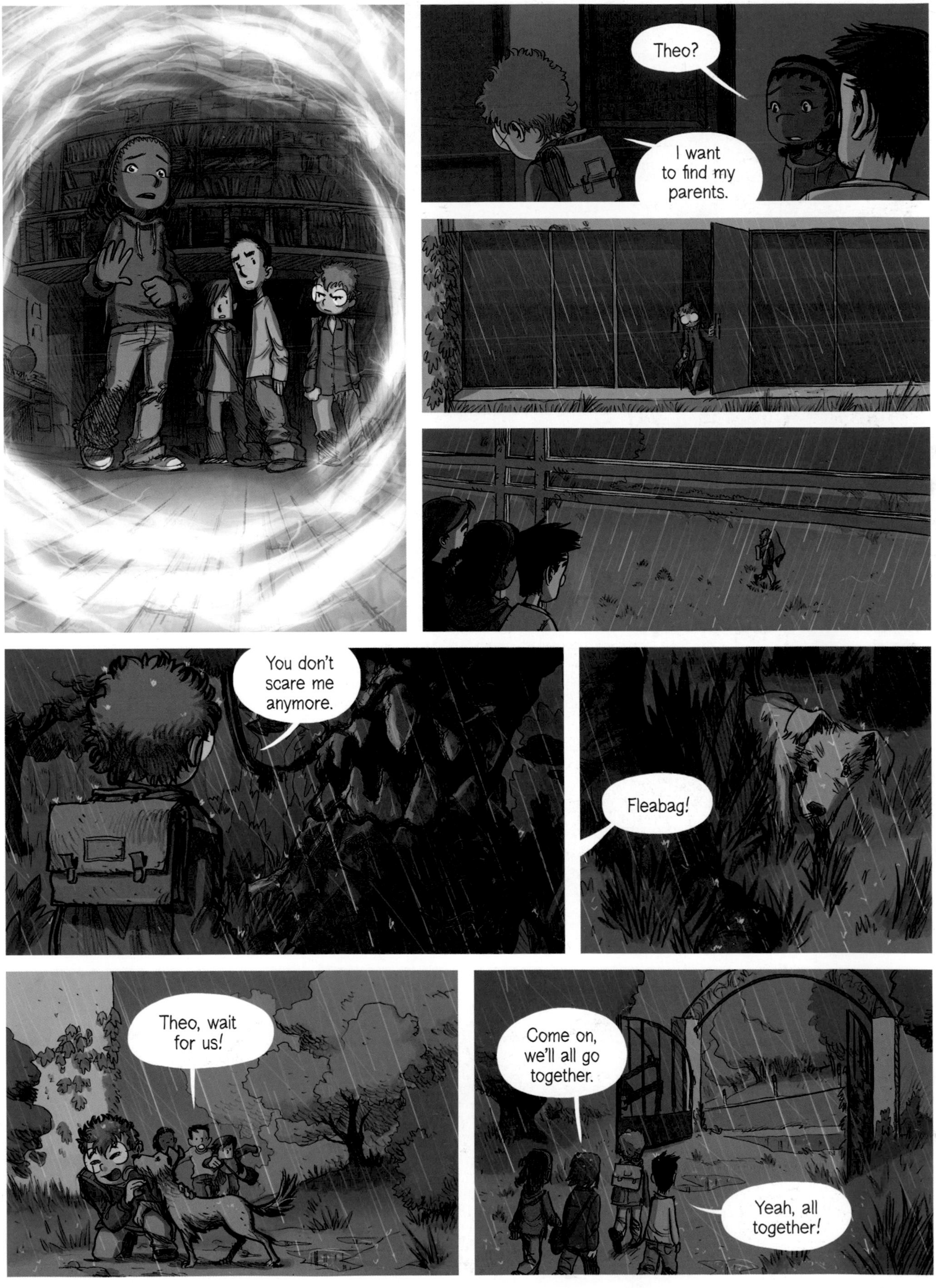
Theo?
I want to find my parents.
You don't scare me anymore.
Fleabag!
Theo, wait for us!
Come on, we'll all go together.
Yeah, all together!

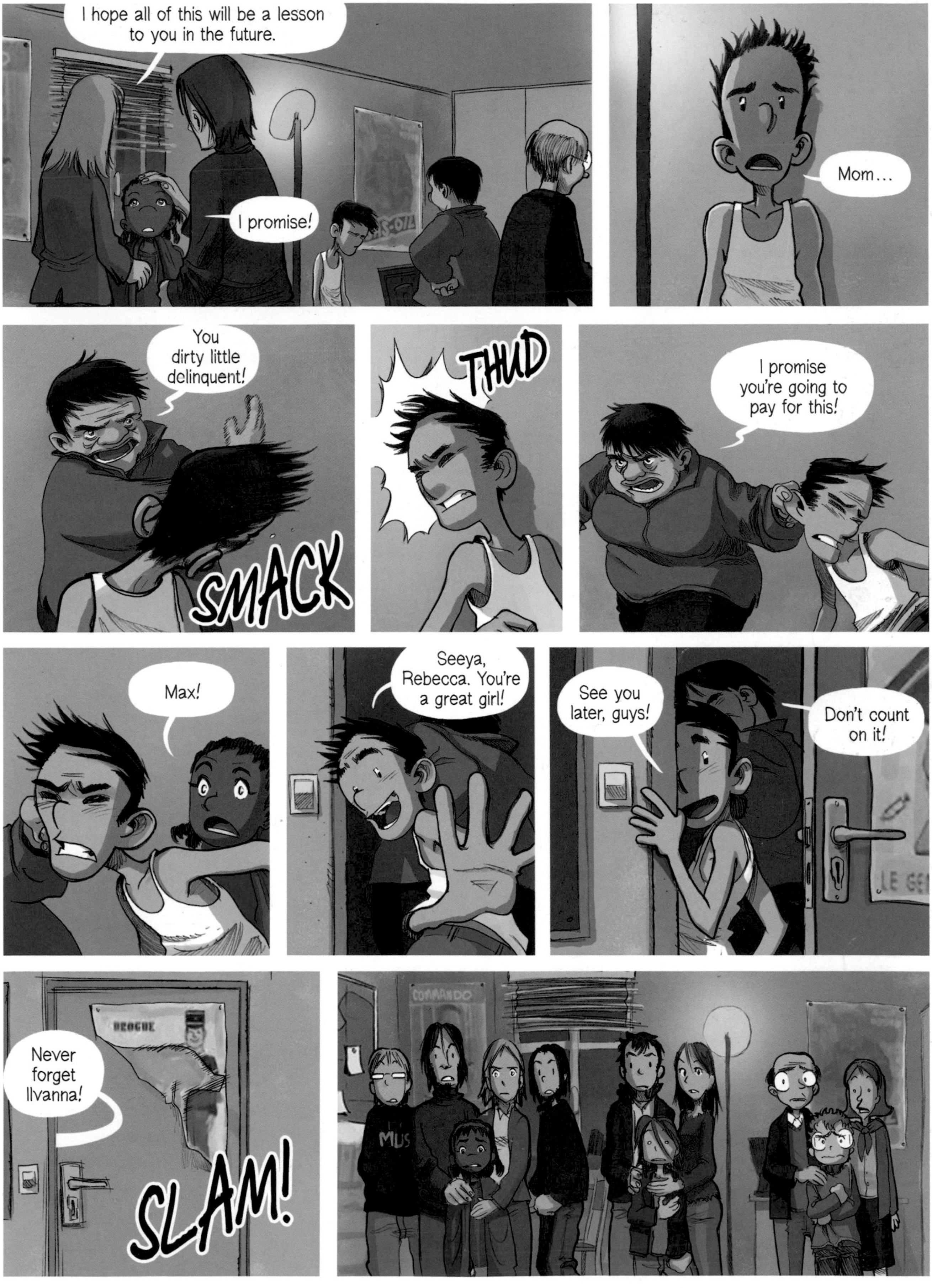
I hope all of this will be a lesson to you in the future.
I promise!
Mom...
You dirty little delinquent!
SMACK
THUD
I promise you're going to pay for this!
Max!
Seeya, Rebecca. You're a great girl!
See you later, guys!
Don't count on it!
Never forget Ilvanna!
SLAM!

four days

The arrest warrant has been lifted on the suspect in this case. Louis Dubbs, better known by the nickname Bruiser. The police captain, Ed Martin, who received congratulations from the chief of police, admitted that the children's explanations have not clarified all the events. He was particularly surprised that they managed to stay hidden for four days in the seaside grotto called Devil's Cave. We remind our readers that Devil's Cave was previously searched with dogs, and no trace of the children was found. To avoid further incidents, the town council has proposed a high fine for trespassing in the

THEO WRIGHT (upper left) MAX TIVELLE (lower left) NOAH WILLIAMS (lower right) and REBECCA DELILLE (above), the survivors of Devil's Cave.

THE MISSING CHILDREN OF PERRYVILLE

Pretending to be shipwrecked children went missing for four days

NEWS IN BRIEF

Shortage of babysitters in Perryville

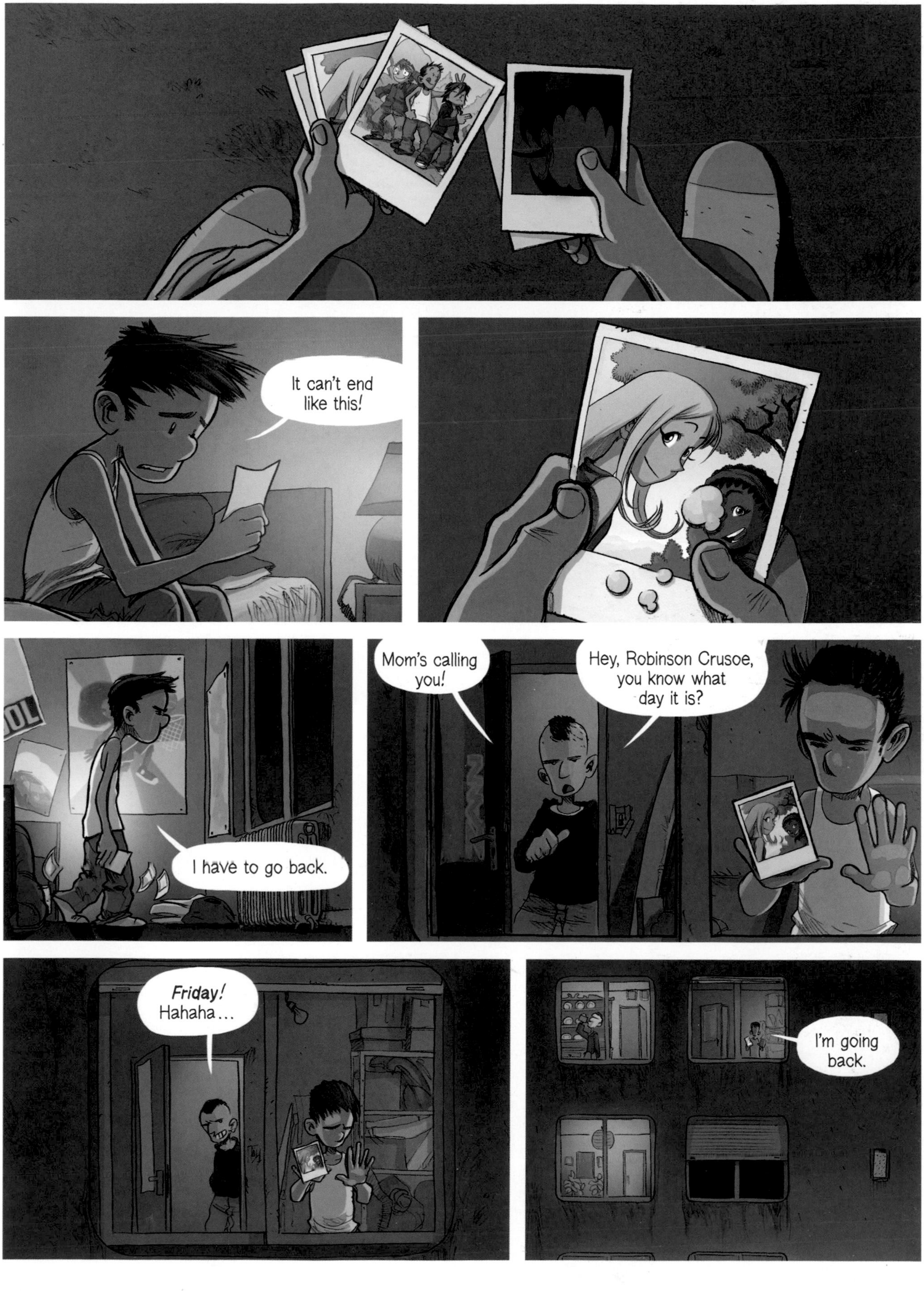
It can't end like this!
I have to go back.
Mom's calling you!
Hey, Robinson Crusoe, you know what day it is?
Friday! Hahaha...
I'm going back.

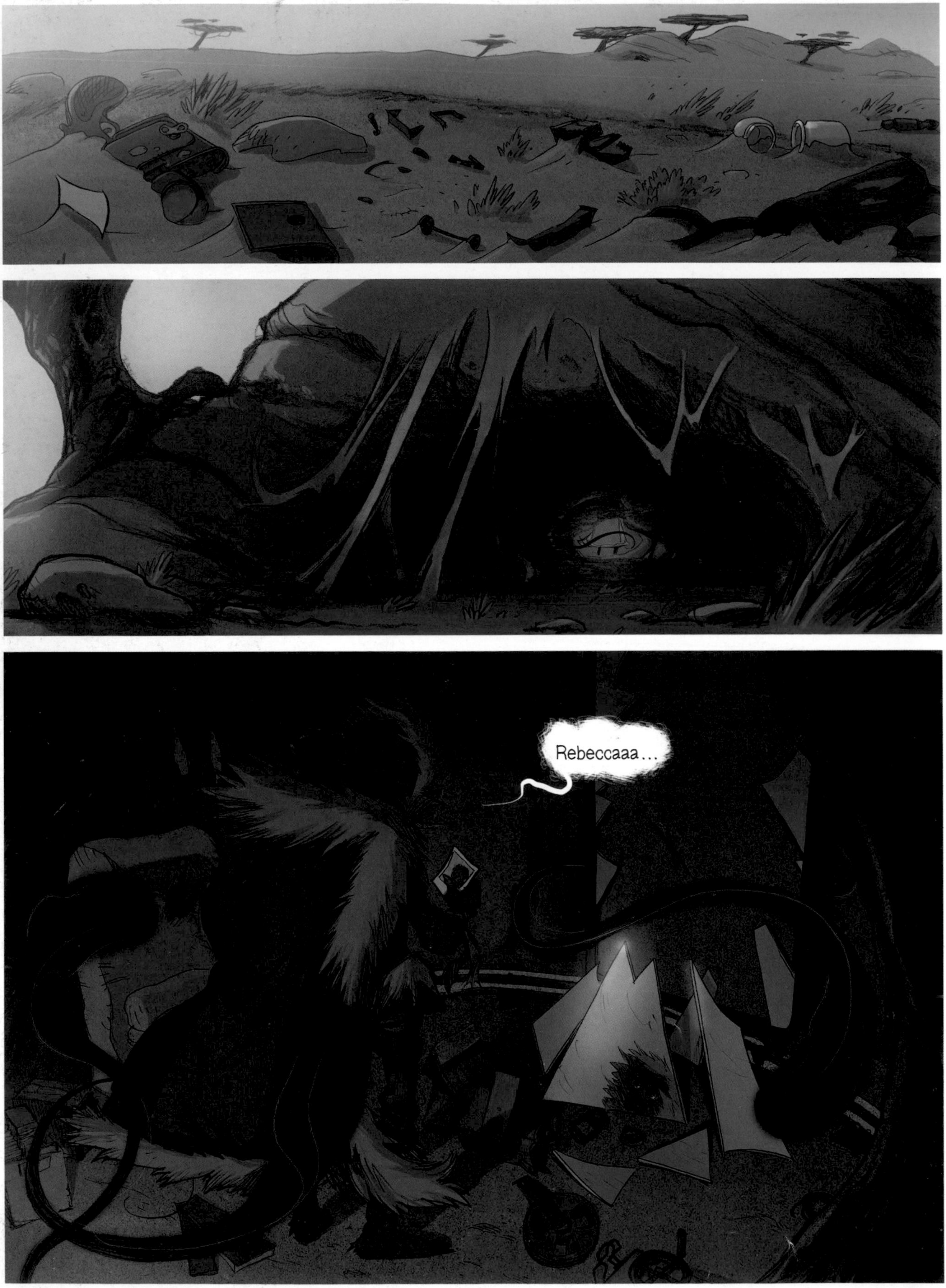
Rebeccaaa...

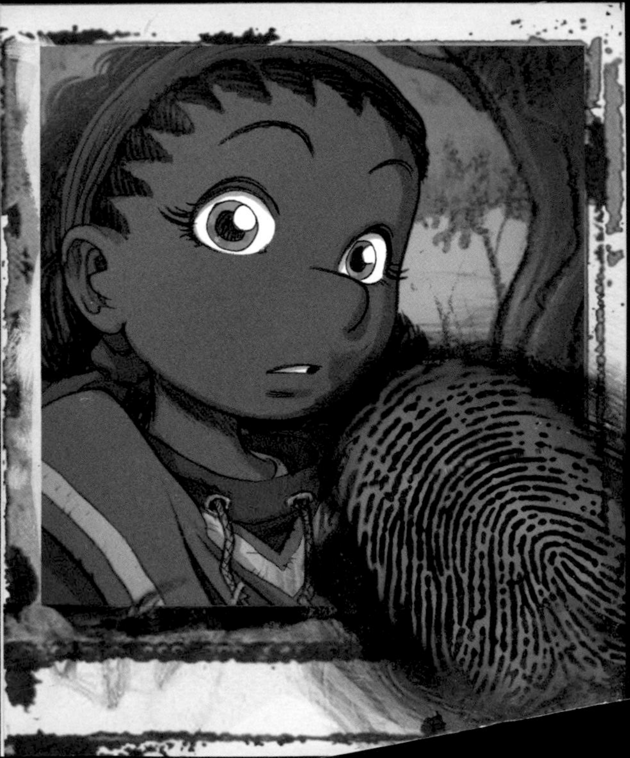

The End ...?

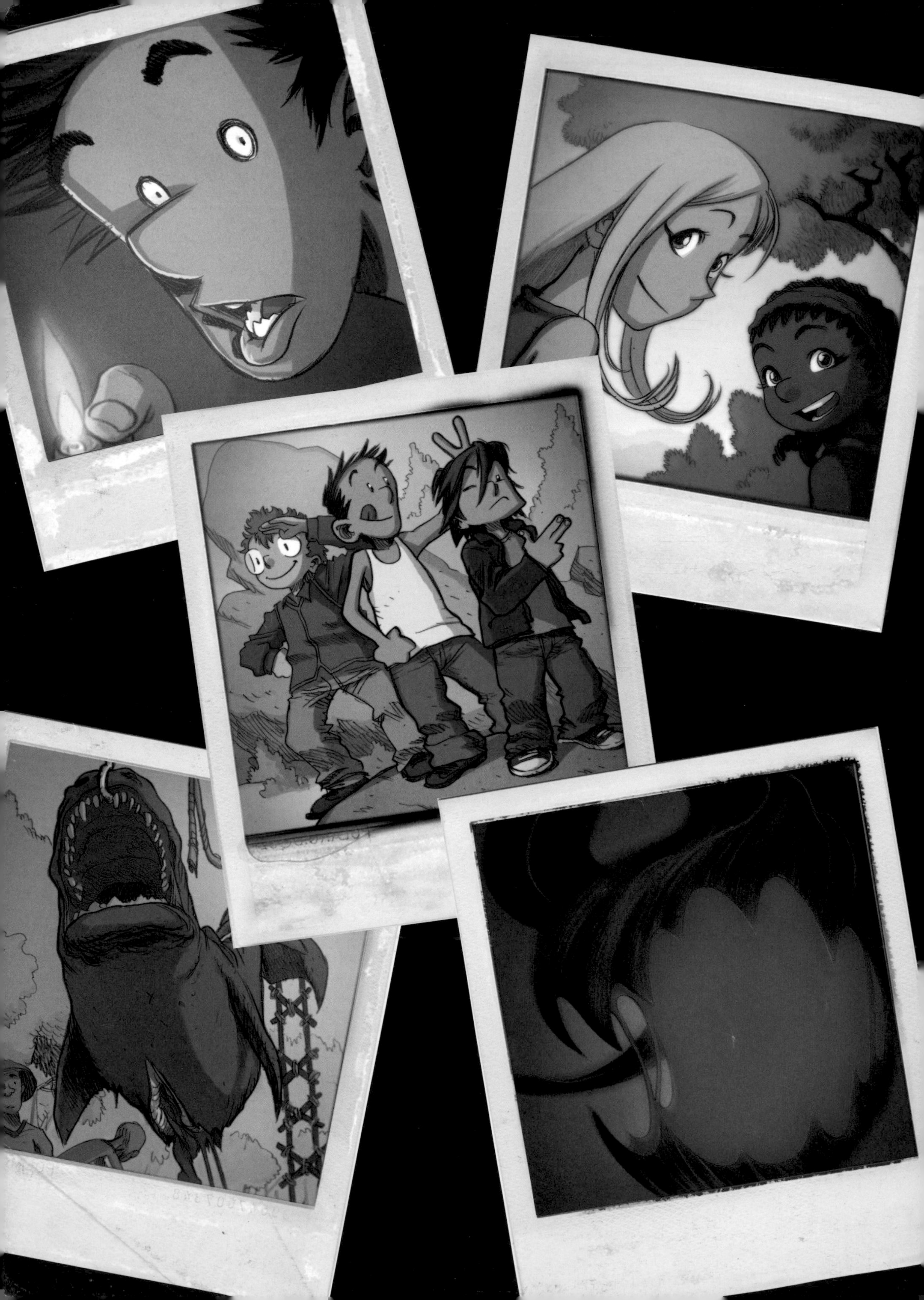

Art by Bannister
Story by Nykko
Colors by Jaffré
Translation by Carol Klio Burrell

First American edition published in 2009 by Graphic Universe™.
Published by arrangement with S.A. DUPUIS, Belgium.

Graphic Universe™
A division of Lerner Publishing Group, Inc.
241 First Avenue North
Minneapolis, MN 55401 U.S.A.

Website address: www.lernerbooks.com

Library of Congress Cataloging-in-Publication Data

Bannister. [Passage. English]
[Maître des ombres. English]
The Master of Shadows / art by Bannister ; story by Nykko ; [colors by Jaffré ;
translation by Carol Klio Burrell]. — 1st American ed.
p.   cm. — (The ElseWhere chronicles ; bk. 3)
Summary: After discovering that Grandpa Gabe has sealed the passageways between
worlds, Max, Rebecca, Theo, and Noah must confront the Master of Shadows himself
to find another way home.
ISBN: 978-0-7613-4461-2 (lib. bdg. : alk. paper)
1. Graphic novels. [1. Graphic novels. 2. Horror stories.] I. Nykko. II. Jaffré. III.
Burrell, Carol Klio. IV. Title.
PZ7.7.B34Mas 2009
741.5'973—dc22   2008039444

Manufactured in the United States of America
1 2 3 4 5 6 - BP - 14 13 12 11 10 09

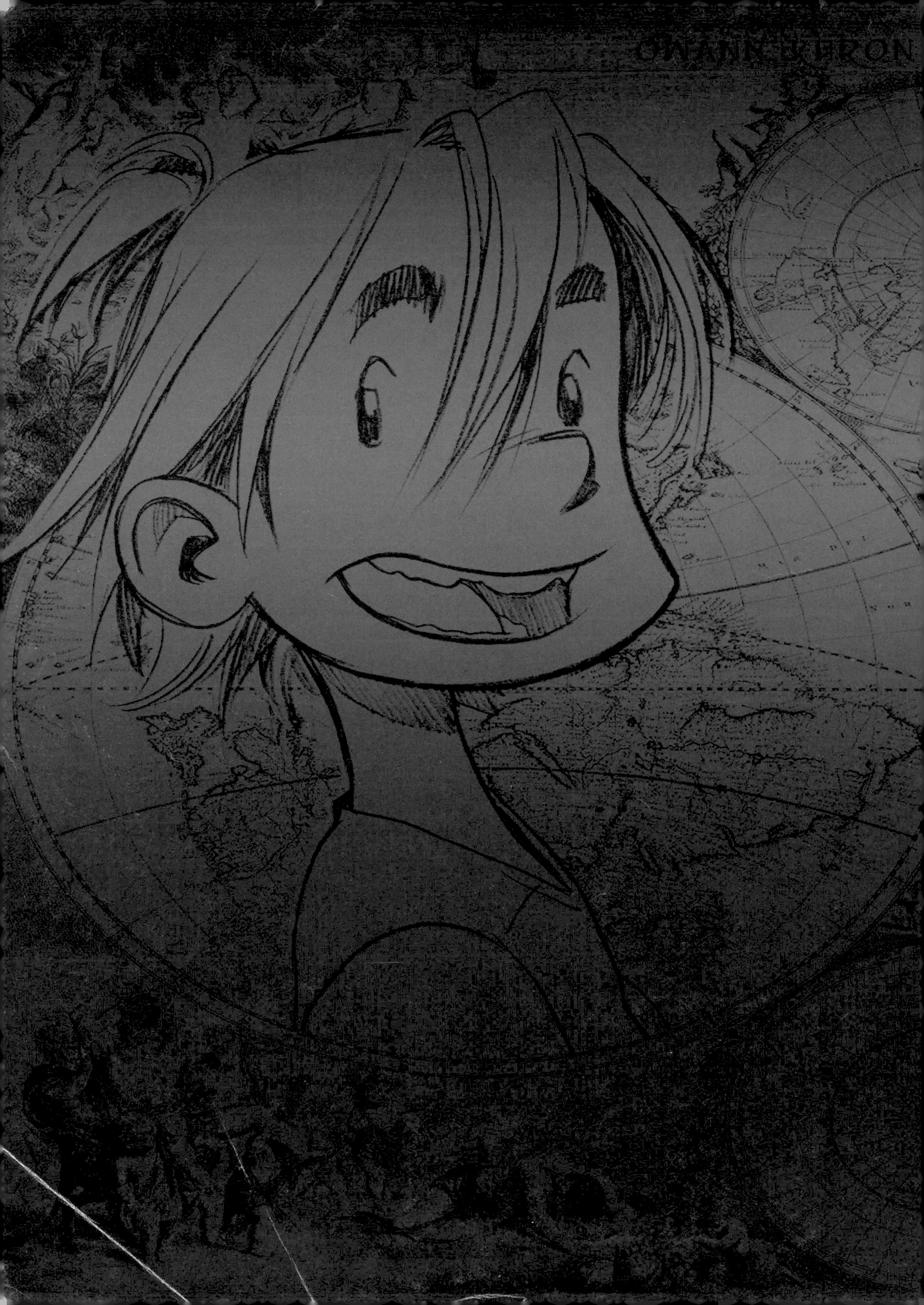